Ejiro

Ejiro

ISRAEL OJIE JOE

origami

Parrésia Publishers Ltd.
82, Allen Avenue, Ikeja, Lagos, Nigeria.
+2348154582178, +2348062392145
origami@parresia.com.ng
www.parresia.com.ng

ISBN: 9789785342574

Printed in Nigeria by Parrésia Press

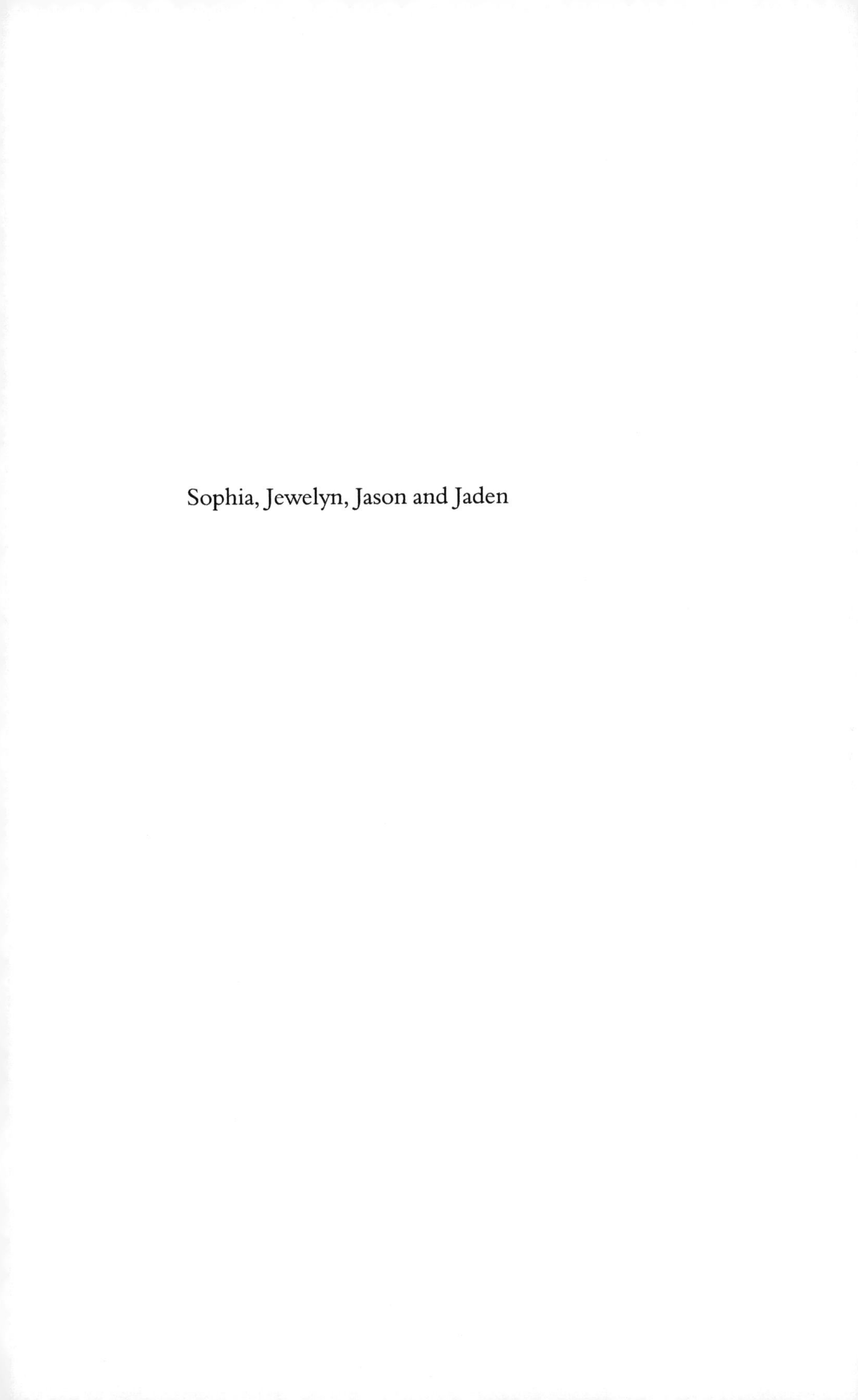

Sophia, Jewelyn, Jason and Jaden

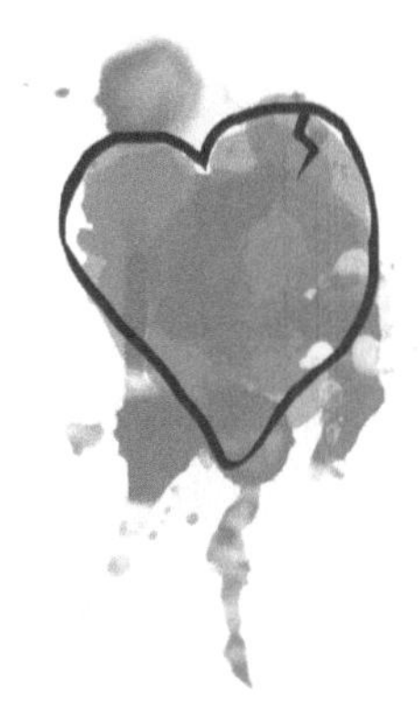

Chapter 1

IT was a golden morning. The sun's orb hung in the sky and sent its rays through the trees lining Campus Avenue. The splendour, which the climate sent, manifested beautifully in my inward. I thought of the sun as God or God as the sun, the same yesterday, today, and every other day. In this mood of peace and curiosity, I spotted an old friend, the second one that morning.

'The sun, indeed, is God,' I thought aloud as I hastened my steps towards her, beckoning cautiously. My mood was a mixture of certainty and doubt.

'Ejiro,' I called tentatively. She turned with a questioning look on her face.

'Yes? Oh, my God! Richard!' she screamed, running towards me. We closed the gap between us and hugged each other.

Ejiro was my first crush, and the only love I knew before her parents got wind of our relationship and sent her away to live with her uncle in Lagos. We were both fourteen. In the following year, I wrote many letters, confessing my love for her and vowing that I would come to find her if she gave me an address. After my eighth letter and still no response, I stopped writing and promised her, in my heart, that I would wait for her till whenever she returned. Now, a decade and a half later, after we had both gone to the university, graduated, and now finding our ways in the world, here she was in the flesh, like a light at the end of a long dark tunnel.

'It's been quite an age,' I said.

'It has,' she responded. 'How have you been? How is Nelly, your brother? What about your parents? How is life?'

'Fine,' I answered the minute I could get a word in. 'Nelly is doing fine. He is a lawyer now, and life is good. We're ploughing on. How are things at your end?'

'Ah, life is great. But you didn't answer the question about your parents?'

'My parents have passed on, Ejiro.'

'Oh my God,' she said, covering her mouth. 'When? What happened? Were they sick? Was it an accident? Did they get help? Did you–?

I wanted to laugh. Ejiro had not changed. She was the one person I knew who showed concern by asking questions after questions without giving time for response. Having exhausted her questions, she would turn on the listener and ask why they were not giving any answers. But I did not laugh. My parents had died a few months after my second year at the university. Nelly, my brother, had just gotten admission into the university. At that time, I did not see a way to survive without them. The pain of knowing that I would never see them again was almost too much to bear. But time does something for pain; it dulls its edges and makes it passable, almost benign.

'Thank you, Ejiro,' I responded. 'They were not sick; they were in an accident. It's been a while now, actually.'

'It is well,' she said.

'So, what brought you here?'

'I am also doing a course.'

'Oh, great,' I responded.

We soon moved into the campus and found a spot where we could sit and do catch up. Ejiro didn't seem in a hurry, and I was eager to listen to her story and have her hear mine.

After Ejiro left Port Harcourt for Lagos, she was sent to a boarding school in a place called Ameda, a somnolent town close to Akure in Ondo State. Her school was reputed to have high standards of academics and moral discipline. And although she survived, she did not bloom. Her ride to the university was not smooth. She struggled with her identity in her new school in Ameda. The other students often gossiped about her in the Yoruba language, not minding that she was there. She could not make friends and had only her books as companions. She studied hard, passed the WAEC and JAMB examinations at her first attempts, and got admission into the University of Ibadan to study Communication and Language Arts. There, she blossomed. She was now at the University of Port Harcourt for her postgraduate.

'But Ejiro, you never responded to my letters.'

'You never wrote,' she countered.

'But I did. I wrote, telling you to give me an address so I would come and rescue you. I promised to wait for you till whenever you came back. I wrote a letter every week for almost one year.'

Ejiro laughed while I said all these things. Presently, she stopped. 'Okay, Richard, I did not get your letters. I wonder why. But I am not laughing at you; I am just laughing at the fervour with which you must have written all those promises, Mr Prince Charming,' she laughed again. 'By the way, which address were you sending the letters to?'

'The address you gave me in Lagos.'

'So, you had the address?'

'Yes.'

'So, why didn't you just come? Why did you need to ask me for the address? Did it not occur to you that you had the address?'

I burst out laughing. I understood the reason for her laughter. I had written to her to give me an address so that I could whisk her away; meanwhile, it was an address I was sending the letters to. It never occurred to me. We both laughed.

There was a twinkle in Ejiro's eyes when she laughed. It was the shine I had always known. It was there every time she smiled, was being mischievous, or planned some derring-do. The twinkle transported me to a distant memory.

I was in JSS 2 at Lord Lugard's College when Ejiro and I first became friends. In teaching the use of conjunctions, our English teacher used the expression, 'Ejiro AND Richard', and that marked the beginning of our friendship.

After class that day, I saw Ejiro being intimidated by Ebi. Ebi was a senior whom everyone feared, including his mates. He was a bully and was brazen about it. I saw him snatch Ejiro's water bottle during lunch one day. I did not think about the consequence before I intervened. I told Ebi that he was a bully and that bullying was wrong. Of course, Ebi turned on me and gave me several knocks on the head, but Ejiro went free. Other senior students, who saw a chance to be friendly with Ebi, added their own bits of punishment— a knock, a slap, an occasional kick. I suffered as Ebi made me cut grass for some days, but I gained a friend in Ejiro. After that day, she often shared her lunch with me. She was bold and pleasant. Our friendship was open and known to everyone, and we were almost always together.

After Ejiro and I became friends, I got to know that Ebi picked on her because she refused to be his girlfriend. He then took it upon himself to torture her into submission. But her defiance grew instead, and now she had an ally in me.

As our friendship blossomed and everyone in the school noticed, Ebi was jealous. He ill-treated me whenever he got the chance. Our mates teased us, and some teachers showed their concern. We were counselled, sometimes threatened, but we remained close. All the efforts to keep us apart drew us closer instead.

Someone must have told Ejiro's parents about our friendship because they called her to order and advised her to stop whatever sort of relationship she had with me. But she defied her parents and defended me before them. All these challenges made our tender feelings develop into a full-blown relationship.

Her family was wealthy. Her father was an oil magnate. Ejiro grew up in a massive and beautiful house, surrounded by a tall fence topped with barbed wire. A bed of flowers sat around the wall like a gift to those of us who could not know the luxury within. The other gift Ejiro's house gave to the community was light. At night, the outside light from their house spilt onto the streets, providing light and shadow for the young and old to do their business – both open and clandestine. She lived a cushioned life at home but had to face harsh realities at school. Her father insisted that she should not make friends with children below their social class. In fact, she was in our school because her father could not bear for her to be far away from home. So, she attended school with us but was not allowed to mix with us.

Unlike Ejiro's parents, my parents were not wealthy. My father did not have a university education, nor did my mother. However, my family had honour and a sense of pride. My parents were generationally upwardly mobile people who did what they could to make sure that their children did better. My father struggled to send me and Nelly, my brother, to Lord Lugard College and then to the University of Nigeria, Nsukka.

Perhaps, I thought, as Ejiro and I sat swapping stories on the grounds of Uniport, that if the teachers and Ebi had known that their persecution and threats served as gestation for the very thing they tried to prevent, they might have tried a little less.

'Ejiro, you never wrote, and you knew my address. Why?'

She was quiet. She looked calm in black denim and her ochre-coloured top. Because of the sun, she had put on a pair of Ray-Ban glasses that covered almost half of her face, so I could not read her eyes. What I couldn't see in her eyes was compensated for by the sight of her curvy body. She had mixed her colours well. The ochre-coloured top matched her skin tone, while the charcoal black denim matched her jet-black hair and sunglasses.

'Richard, are you done checking me out?'

'What do you mean? I said you never wrote.'

'And I said, are you done checking me out?'

Chapter 2

KELVIN and I sat in his car as his driver cruised from Campus Avenue to Abuloma, Port Harcourt. We were on our way to his hotel, where we'd sit down and talk. He was my closest friend while we were at the university. He was the first friend I met that morning. We had run into each other as I was heading for a job interview at a bank. We didn't have time to talk then, but we exchanged phone numbers and I promised to call him after my interview. We both studied Mechanical Engineering in UNN and had big dreams of working for the oil corporations that dotted the Niger-Delta landscape like landmines in a time of war.

He was the child of a Sierra-Leonean diplomat who was posted to Nigeria. His parents were wealthy and had access to everything the Nigerian upper-class played with. Kelvin was one of the richest students on campus, but he was not loud and extravagant. His parents had drilled into him a sense of self-worth that was not dependent on the things he had. Even though Kelvin had access to money, cars, and a security detail who doubled as his driver, he strove hard to live a normal life on campus. He did not stay in the school halls of residence, and only a few people knew where he stayed. Not many people knew that his parents were diplomats. They assumed he was another rich student with a car and a driver.

The way Kelvin and I became friends is a story that is not so interesting. I was on my way to the Engineering block to check the notice board when it suddenly began to rain. I had no money, so I could not take the campus shuttle. When the rain started, I knew I would get soaked, but I plodded on. And just as I was about to cross the road to enter the school campus, a vehicle sped up from behind me and splashed water on my clothes. Perhaps it wasn't intentional, but I had no way of knowing as the driver did not stop. I continued my journey after silently cursing the car and its owner.

When I finally made it to the board, there was a crowd. And just outside the building was the car which splashed water on me earlier. I decided that before going in, I'd settle a score. I walked to the car and knocked on its window. As the driver wound down, I accused him of messing up my shirt and not deeming it fit to stop to apologise. The driver did not utter a word after I was done with my ranting; he simply sat there looking at me. I was about to lose my cool when he bounded out. I took two steps backwards, thinking he was going to hit me, but he went to open the door. I collided with his boss.

'I am sorry about what happened earlier,' he said.

'See,' I said, facing the driver. 'That's how good people behave. He just apologised; you didn't.'

Kelvin apologised again and explained that he had told the driver to speed up. He asked what I was doing there, and I told him that I came to check my results.

'Wait, are you in Mech Engine?' he asked.

'Yes. You?'

'Same. What level?'

'200. I came to check the faculty broadsheet. I heard that our 100 level GP has been calculated.'

'Let's go check,' he said.

It turned out that my grades were outstanding, and Kelvin's were not bad either. We decided there and then that we should form a partnership, his strength compensating for my weakness and vice versa.

Our friendship blossomed, and Kelvin and I grew very close. My relationship with Kelvin made it so that I never lacked for anything. Kelvin had enough and lots more to spare. I worried less about funds and could focus on my academics. Even my brother had some measure of comfort.

Soon enough, I was at the receiving end of other students' jealousy. Everything that could not get to Kelvin because he seemed to live in a bubble got to me. No matter how much time I spent with Kelvin, I had to return to the hostel and my colleagues. When people saw that teasing me did not work, they approached me to get Kelvin to do something for them. Some people wanted money; some people wanted him to be friends with them too. But I knew my limits and tried not to interfere in Kelvin's private life.

It took a while, but other students soon found out that they could not get me to make Kelvin do their bidding. So, they left me alone and tried to reach him themselves. But Kelvin had constructed a wall around himself. Not many students knew where he lived. When not in a class, he was with his driver who doubled as his security guard. He never partied, at least not among students, and he maintained a very strict schedule that seldom left time for interruptions.

Soon, it was time to graduate. I finished with a First Class and as the best student in the faculty, while Kelvin made a second class higher division. I hoped that my grade would open doors of employment for me very quickly, and life would soon take shape.

I had many questions on my mind as Kelvin and I reached his hotel and settled in his room. How had he been? What was he doing in Nigeria? Sierra Leone had a new president, and the name sounded like his father's. Was his father now the President of Sierra Leone? But he was the one who asked the first question.

'So, tell me, Riche, why did you never get in touch? My sister never stopped talking about you. She said you promised to call, but you never did. It was like you turned your back on me after you left Sierra Leone. I tried to reach you, but all my efforts came to nought. What happened?'

I had gone to Sierra Leone on Kelvin's father's invitation. His family had organised a party for his graduation and wanted me to be there. Kelvin helped me to process my travel documents and paid for my flight to Freetown. At the airport, a car was waiting to take me to his family house, where the party would hold the next day. I had an amazing time with them. He had told his parents that his academic success was a result of our friendship. I tried to deflect this praise by saying that we had encouraged each other to work hard, but his parents were insistent on their thanks and asked me to name anything they could do for me. I thanked them and told them I would be in touch.

Kelvin's younger sister had taken a shine to me during my week-long stay in Kelvin's family house. She followed me about and went with me as Kelvin took me around the country. She asked me many questions about growing up in Nigeria and how it felt to have graduated with a First Class. I tried to answer the questions as honestly as possible. When she asked about my parents, I gave a wry smile. She did not press the question. I told her they were no more. She showed sympathy and encouraged me to be the master of my best self. Kelvin's father offered to get me a job if I stayed in Sierra Leone. Again, I thanked them all and told them I would be in touch.

Things went awry when I touched down in Nigeria. After

checking out my baggage, I lost most of it to airport touts who wanted to help me get a cab. Hard as I tried, I never found the touts or my luggage. Perhaps I should have known I wasn't in for a smooth post-campus life when I lost my phone and valuables at the airport. I had no way of reaching Kelvin or his sister or anyone in Sierra Leone. I made it home with the money in my pocket. I tried contacting a few people who knew Kelvin to get his number, but they did not have his Sierra Leonean mobile number. I tried using social media but to no avail. I went to the Admissions and Records office at UNN, hoping that I would get any helpful information, but the people at the office had looked at me cross-eyed and told me they were not at liberty to divulge personal information to outsiders.

'Richard, we looked for you. I tried your phone, but it did not connect. My sister pined for you. I did not know you had made quite an impression on her during your brief stay with us.'

'Where is she now?'

'The US, Harvard. Studying to be a doctor.'

'Oh, great! She is brainy.'

'Yes, Riche, she is. She is engaged now. You broke her heart, man, but she has gotten over it.'

It had been an interesting day so far. In one morning, I ran into two old friends in Port Harcourt. First, Ejiro; now Kelvin. I was on my way to my aunt's house to get some money for my upkeep. I could not secure a job and sometimes had to depend on my aunt's magnanimity to survive. Upon graduation, it turned out that a First-Class grade was inadequate without knowing someone who knew someone who knew someone else. Working in the oil companies was like joining an exclusive club – one could not get in without recommendation. But I kept applying, and I had just been invited to a second stage interview at Supreme Oil and Gas.

'So, Riche, what's up? What are you doing now?'

I told Kelvin I was still job hunting.

'Oh, my God!'

'What? Are you mocking me? All these oil companies we thought we'd breeze into always ask for ten years' experience. Some of them ask for five years' experience, and they still want you to be below twenty-eight years. In fact, they are mostly interested in employing people who schooled abroad,' I had spoken vehemently.

'Richard,' Kelvin said gently. 'I am not mocking you; I would never do that. But I wish you had made contact. I wish you had reached out. My parents could have helped, especially now that my father is the president.'

I looked up sharply.

'Yes, Richard. My father contested and won the presidential elections in Sierra Leone. In fact, I am in Nigeria on business. My company won the contract to build some roads in Sierra Leone, and I am here to source materials for the project.'

Richard told me about his life as a president's son, the opportunities that came his way, and how he handled them. I told him about the interviews and tests I had attended in my search for a job. I informed him that I had been invited to the second stage of the interview with Supreme Oil and Gas. He congratulated me and wished me luck. We talked some more, and after we had lunch, I rose to leave.

'I need to get to my aunt's house.'

'Oh! Aunty Rose?'

'Yes,' I said.

'Oh, great! I should come with you. I don't want you out of my sight anymore before you disappear for another five years.'

Aunty Rose was my father's younger sister. Like my father, she had grown up poor and learnt to struggle and fend for herself early in life. But she had married up. She married a white man and had gone to realise her dream of becoming a lawyer. My aunt was a brilliant lawyer who had offices in Port Harcourt and Lagos. She often crisscrossed the country to defend her clients. She attributed her success at law to going to school late and her ability to quickly decipher things that puzzled youngsters. The things that seem like disadvantages, she once said, are blessings in formation.

Kelvin and I got to Aunty Rose's house late in the afternoon. The sun had by then lost its sharp edge and left us with its retreating colour. It was a breezy evening; the type perfect for a stroll. One might go for a run with ear-buds plugged in, share his heart with a loved one, or perhaps visit family and friends like I was doing.

The sun's yellow hue accentuated the colour of everything in Aunty Rose's compound. The compound was dotted with flowers: Ixora, Hibiscus, Bougainvillea, and Roses. The building itself was a sturdy bungalow built with red bricks. Inside, I knew I would be confronted with art pieces ranging from small figurines to medium-sized paintings. Her wall was dotted with plaques and family pictures of herself, her husband, and her two sons, my cousins. There was also a chandelier that did not fail to arrest a visitor's attention. The dominant smell inside the house was a cross between roses and saltpetre. I was showing Kelvin my favourite figurine when my aunt came in.

'Good afternoon, aunty.'

'Hello, Richard,' she said. 'Is that how to greet your aunt? Loving me from afar? Come here and give me a hug, naughty boy.'

I walked up to her and embraced her.

'No matter how big you get, you are still my baby.'

I nodded and introduced Kelvin. 'Aunty, this is Kelvin, my friend from the university.'

'Oh, I remember him! The one from Sierra Leone. How are you, my young man?'

'I am fine, ma'am,' Kelvin responded.

'I am sure life is good?'

'Yes, aunty. Thank you. Nice place you have here. Richard was just showing me his favourite pieces.'

'Oh, thank you. Thank you very much.'

Aunty Rose turned to go back to the kitchen. 'Let me get you something to eat.'

'No, aunty. We had lunch not too long ago,' I said.

'Oh, you did? You were coming to my house, and you had lunch?'

There was mock anger on her face. It was nothing serious, but I knew my aunt liked to do things for my brother and me. Since our parents died, she had done everything possible to make sure we were comfortable. She had played the role of both parents in our lives, paying our fees and doing her best to make sure we lacked for nothing. Now that I was out of university and had no job, she had not nagged me for one day. She had done what she could to encourage me to keep trying, not to stop hoping. Now she asked me why I had the temerity to eat lunch when I knew I was coming to her house.

'Aunty, I am sorry. I ran into Kelvin today, and we tried to catch up over lunch.'

'Okay,' she said. 'Let me get you water or juice.'

Kelvin responded, 'We are really filled up, ma.'

'Okay, then. I'll pack you some food to take away. You boys need to eat more, especially this one,' she pointed at me.

'You,' she pointed at Kelvin. 'I see a woman's hands on you. Is she your wife or your mother?'

Kelvin smiled in response. Aunty Rose smiled too and bustled into the kitchen to give the cook instructions. When she came back, she put on a video. It was one of the latest Nollywood movies.

'Aunty,' I called. 'Can I see you briefly, ma?'

'Yes, sure.'

I excused myself from Kelvin, but he waved me away. He was engrossed in the movie showing on the TV.

I informed Aunty Rose that I had an interview at Supreme Oil and Gas. I pleaded with her to lend me fifteen thousand Naira, but Aunty Rose rebuffed me. She warned me never to ask to borrow money from her again; if I needed anything, I should just ask. She said she hoped I got a job soon so I could regain my self-esteem and stop thinking I had no right to make demands on the world, my family included. After scolding me, she transferred seventy-five thousand Naira to my bank account.

Chapter 3

'**SO**,' Kelvin tapped me. 'Riche, what's up with this Ejiro you are always talking to on the phone?'

Since the day we ran into each other at Uniport, Kelvin and I saw every day. He spent his days attending meetings and his evenings with me. We had quite a lot to catch up on. Kelvin was married and already had one child, and another was on the way. But he still loved a good story; he still liked to talk politics, argue about football, and talk about girls.

Asking this question now, I saw a smile tug at the sides of his mouth. From experience, I knew this was a preface to some sarcastic comment. I decided to come clean.

'Ejiro was my first crush. We grew up together, but she relocated to Lagos while we were in secondary school and we lost touch. Now she has resurfaced, and I feel the need to reconnect, that's all.'

'Reconnect?'

'Yes. Nothing is wrong with that now, is there?'

Kelvin made a face. 'Am I missing something?'

'Okay, I don't know where this will lead, but we are picking up our friendship. She has even invited me to her house.'

'Wait,' Kelvin's eyes went wide. 'She asked you over?'

'Yes.'

'Where does she live?'

'Lagos.'

'Lagos? Did she invite you to Lagos? That is some serious stuff.'

I shrugged.

'When do you want to go?'

'Saturday. I'll take the night bus and arrive on Saturday morning. I can see her by evening and return the next day.'

'No, no, no, no. None of that,' Kelvin said. 'Lagos is far, and it is too risky to travel by night. With the killings of herdsmen, boko haram, kidnappings on the highways, bandits attacks and Biafra self-determination, you still contemplate traveling at night? This should be the worse thought at this moment before the security agents works on it to make the road safer. By the way, how will you get to Lagos?'

'I have some money,' I said.

'Wait, Richard. This girl invites you to Lagos, you want to put everything aside and go to Lagos, and you are telling me you just want to reconnect? You are supposed to be prepping for an interview with Supreme Oil.'

I cocked my head at an angle and smiled.

'There definitely is something to this that you are not telling me. What kind of reconnection is this?' Kelvin made a face, but he was about to burst into laughter and I saw it. 'Anyway, you won't need to go by night bus. You'll go by air, and I am coming with you.'

'Kelvin, air travel is expensive.'

'Who said you were going to pay?'

I knew what Kelvin was trying to say, and I didn't like the idea. Kelvin had supported me throughout the university, and it seemed like those days were about to happen again. I thought there had to be something to show for the passage of time. Why do I have to receive favour again from the same man from whom I received them steadily some years ago?

'Thanks, Kelvin,' I said. 'I appreciate your kind gesture, but I really need to do this on my own.'

'Come on, Richard. Let me come with you. Besides, I have a meeting in Lagos this weekend.'

'Okay,' I relented. 'We can go on the early morning flight on Saturday. But I am only letting you do this because you have a business in Lagos yourself.'

Kelvin dropped me at home around 6pm. that day. He did not come in because he had a meeting with one of the steel consortiums in Port Harcourt, and he did not want to be late.

As soon as I stepped into the two-bedroom apartment I shared with Nelly, my brother, I went straight to the bathroom for a shower. I tried to process the events of the last three days. Nothing went as planned, yet everything had gone wonderfully well. I met an old love and discovered that I still cared about her. I ran into a buddy and we were renewing our friendship. When my phone rang, I was already in bed, but I answered it. It was Kelvin. He had returned to his hotel and wanted my full name the way it appeared on my ID. As soon as we ended the call, I fell into a long sleep punctuated by dreams.

It is often said that dreams come from three sources: God, Satan, and a multitude of businesses. I must have had a million dreams that night, all of which came from the latter. Some of my dreams reached into the past when Kelvin and I were students at UNN, while a few stretched into the future, a prediction of the near future based on my present realities. Of all the dreams I had that night, one seemed like a perfect re-enactment of a moment I shared with Kelvin.

> *Kelvin and I go to a fancy restaurant. Once we parked our car, Kelvin walks ahead of me into the restaurant. While walking behind him, I notice his body. He has filled out, thanks to regular feeding and peace of mind. I recall my aunt's question: 'I can see a woman's hands on you. Who is she, your wife or your mother?' So, when we settle down, I ask him to tell me the story of how he met his wife. Instead, he turns serious and asks me, 'So, you really don't have a job?' I respond in the affirmative. I tell him my job-hunting stories; how sometimes the first question interviewers ask is to know who sent me. Usually, if I could not produce a note or a business card, they check for my name on a list. If they didn't find it, the interview went on. But I always felt there was no force behind it, that it went on out of civility. I tell Kelvin I have another interview with an oil company. Kelvin tells me to do my best at the interview, that he knows some people there and will make some calls. Suddenly, Kelvin is a pilot, and he is making an announcement instead of a call. Then he transforms into an officiating minister who says I may now kiss the bride. I am about to kiss Ejiro when a shrill sound comes on and startles me out of the church!*

I woke up to the shrill sound of my alarm. It was 4:45 am. The alarm clock was a gift that Aunty Rose's husband brought back from an overseas trip. I treasured the alarm clock and put it far out of arm's reach so that I wouldn't one day be angry and fling it across the room. Once it rang, I had to get up to turn it off. Once I got up, I had conquered sleep and my day would begin. I woke up tired. But it was hardly surprising because I had quite a bit to eat and drink with Kelvin the previous evening. The combination of joy and alcohol had a toll on my system. I sat up, thankful that I was not hung over.

It was a bright morning. I had heard arguments and counter-arguments about shorter days and longer nights, but I was not clear. One thing I was sure of was that mornings close to the end of the year were often cold and hazy. However, I could not speak with certainty about the quality of nights close to the end of the year. As I started my day, the remnants of the other dreams seeped into my consciousness. In one dream, Kelvin turned into the CEO of Supreme Oil and asked me where I had been; that a job had been waiting for me all the while. In another dream, Aunty Rose gave me some money and asked me to introduce her to the President of Sierra Leone. I took the money and introduced her to Juliet, Kelvin's sister.

I got out of bed and started preparing for my trip to Lagos. I was going to see Ejiro, my Ejiro, the dreams of my childhood; the one whom I had shared many secrets and fantasies with; the same girl who refused to fade from my consciousness even after we had been separated by time and distance. Ejiro, my Ejiro, now a woman in her own right. Ejiro had invited me to Lagos. Kelvin was right; something was afoot. But did Ejiro know that I had no job? What would happen if she knew? What would I find in Lagos?

I was thinking about all these when I ambled into the sitting room. The place was silent, not strange for that time of the day. A dark form sat facing the wall. For a minute, I thought that a figure from my dreams had somehow escaped into my reality or that I had woken up and not shed the eyesight of dreams. Whatever it was, I was drawn to it. I made to switch on the light.

'Don't turn on the light.'

I froze, then thawed. It was my brother, Nelly. But something was not right because he sounded broken. And why was he sitting down in the dark, facing the wall? I pressed the light switch.

Nelly was a mess. He sat in his work clothes, a now rumpled white shirt, and a black pair of trousers. His polka-dot tie hung low around his neck. His shoes lay on their sides not far away. He still had his socks on. He must have sat there all night but dozed off at some point because he had drooled all over his shirt. Now he had woken up to his sorrow.

'Nelly,' I called. 'What is the matter? Ogini?'

Nelly held out an envelope. I knew it had something to do with work.

'You were sacked?' I asked.

He had said nothing about having trouble at work. Nelly worked in Aunty Rose's law office as a counsel. It was her way of showing him the ropes about how law worked in the real world. I took the envelope and opened it. It contained a wedding invitation and a letter.

'She dumped me.'

'Who? Lilian?'

Nelly nodded.

'What happened? You guys had a fight?'

Tears dropped from my brother's eyes. Nelly and I were very close. We had been that way since we were children. We knew each other's friends, told each other our secrets, and worked through our disappointments together. Nelly had witnessed my distress at not getting a job despite having graduated with a First Class and as the best student in my department. He was there when I lamented that I was jinxed because I had lost Kelvin's contact. I, too, had witnessed his many anguished moments at his job and his agonies over his girlfriends. He had gone through a complete cycle of girlfriends before settling for Lilian. There was a time when she was the sun that rose and fell in his life. It was clear that it was a marriage-facing relationship from the very beginning. However, Nelly had often complained about Lillian's taste for expensive things and her love for high-end fun places. He had once tried to talk her into living within their means, but she had not budged.

Once, when I chatted with Lilian, she told me that Nelly was too conservative and wanted him to switch things up a bit. I had sent a smiling emoji and encouraged her to bear with him and try to work things out. Obviously, they hadn't.

'Nelly, did you guys fight?'

'No, Richard.' Nelly's voice did little to mask his brokenness. 'Lilian and I didn't fight.'

'So, this just happened?'

'She sent this to me via a friend. Actually, I noticed that our relationship was growing distant, and we were not talking as we used to. When I asked, she told me not to worry that she was working on some things. She said I would know when she was done.'

'And then you get this?'

'Richard, this is what I get for trying to be loyal.' Nelly's sorrow turned to bitterness and anger. 'The bloody coward, why couldn't she face me? Why did she have to send this through a friend?'

'Please take it easy,' I said. I did not know what else to say. It is bad enough when a lover breaks up with you, but to send you a wedding invitation without disagreement or any indication was worse. It was spite.

'Riche, we did not fight; we did not argue. How long has this been going on? Why has this girl been deceiving me?'

I kept mute. I recalled how Nelly had invested his emotions, time, and resources into his relationship with Lilian. I also knew how Lilian had been loving but sometimes threatened to break up the engagement. It seemed to me that the red lights had been there all along. Why didn't Nelly see it? But what really bothered me now was what he was going to do.

'Have you spoken to her?' I asked.

'She hasn't been picking my calls. I saw her four days ago. Although I felt that she was acting kind of strange during our time together. She was all flighty and uptight. But since we did not fight and our relationship had survived much more, I did not fret.'

'Ndo. O ga dim ma.'

I took the envelope, and it was then that I saw that it contained something else - a picture of Lilian and an angry-looking man. It became apparent to me that this was a taunt. Why did she include the picture? Why does one step on an already fallen person? I decided to hold on to it; better to get the source of misery out of sight.

'My heart is broken into pieces,' Nelly said. 'I don't know what to do.'

I sighed. 'Nelly, put yourself together. I know it is hard, but you have to move on. A breakup is painful, but it is not the end of life. It's not a reason to fall sick, avoid people, or even take revenge. And God forbid you to think of harming yourself. When things happen like this, it might be the turning point you need. Look, Nelly, this girl has shown you very clearly that she has been playing games with you. It is not worth it that you put your life on hold for her.'

'Richard, I love that girl. I was hoping we could work things out, that we would get married.'

'Nelly, I know. But with what has happened, do you think she loved you?'

Silence.

'Nelly,' I said, gently now. 'I know you are sore. But this girl had moved on before you even knew to stop. Please, Nwannem, rouse yourself and carry on with your life.'

Nelly was quiet, but I could see the light come into his eyes beneath the brokenness. I decided to press home my point. My voice became slightly upbeat.

'You can't keep being sad because of anyone, especially if that person is going to be happy regardless of your pain. Rise, Nelly,' I demonstrated, hoping to get him to laugh. 'Good things will happen to you yet.'

Nelly smiled tentatively. So, I joked with him and tried to get him to go out. Before long, we were talking about Kelvin and my trip to Lagos with him. I got Nelly to promise to invite his friends over or go to them. A little beer does a broken heart well. My opinion.

I stood up to prepare too. One and a half hour had passed since I walked into the sitting room and met a shadow against the dawn. I thought, as I packed my bag, that sorrow comes to all and sundry. It comes to the young because they are naïve. They ask questions about it and spend a better time of their lives looking for answers. To the old, sorrow comes as a by-product of experience; it is sometimes couched as regret.

I hurried with my preparation. Kelvin would soon be here. I got dressed and started to make breakfast. Nelly had also cleaned up the sitting room and put himself together. He was not his usual chatty self yet, but he was well on the way. I was eating when a knock sounded on the door.

'Who is that?' Nelly answered.

'Who is who?' the caller asked. 'Come and open this door, my friend.'

Nelly opened the door. 'Ah, Kelvin. It is truly you. When Richard told me you were around and coming here today, I thought he was hallucinating.'

They shook hands.

'Hi, Nelly. How is it going?'

'I am fine, Kelvin. How is life? Though I am angry with you. You have been seeing Riche these past few days, and you did not even bother to come here.'

'Sorry, Nelly. I have been busy with business meetings. I am sorry I didn't come here. But I am here now.'

'So it is. Good to see you. And you look well.'

'Thank you, Nelly. You don't look bad yourself.'

Kelvin sat. He glanced briefly at me and smiled. I raised my fork at him and asked him to come over to the table for some food.

'No, thanks,' he said. 'I had breakfast at the hotel.'

I nodded.

'So, Richard told me you both are going to Lagos,' Nelly said.

'Yes, we are. And if he doesn't finish that food and get us moving in the next five minutes, we'll miss our flight.'

I looked up and waved the fork again. They both burst into laughter.

'Richard, I wonder how you can eat after all we ate yesterday.'

'Kelvin, my brother, to each day his own. Even the good book says, 'Give us this day our daily bread.' 'Ride on, Pastor,' Nelly said.

Everyone laughed. I got up and ran into my room to get my bag, and we got ready to leave.

'Stay well, Nelly,' I said. 'Look after yourself.'

'Okay,' he responded.

We headed outside the house where Kelvin had a cab waiting. As we left the house, I thought the situation was ironic. Nelly had lost a relationship, and I was on my way to rekindle the fire of an old flame.

Chapter 4

THE road to Port Harcourt International Airport tells a story of its own. Depending on where you are coming from, you are likely to see a transformation from pothole-riddled roads to smooth roads in the neighbourhood of the airport. It often amused me that the rich chose to live in the shadow of aeroplanes. Perhaps, I thought, it reminded them that they could leave anytime they decided, that the portal of escape was just next door.

The taxi that took Kelvin and me to the airport was the same one that had carried us around since the day I met Kelvin. He had contacted the man who had been his driver cum bodyguard while we were in school to drive him around for the duration of his stay in Port Harcourt. It was good. It gave the man a chance to have a steady regular client for a few days. Maybe it robbed him of the opportunity to attract a new clientele. But I knew that it was better for the average Nigerian business owner to have one client that one was sure of than to risk losing him in the hope of a better come-along. No one traded in hope anymore. Everyone dealt with the present. It becomes even better if one could secure the future with the present.

Once we arrived, we went into the domestic wing of the airport. Kelvin and I meandered through the crowd until we got to the boarding area where the Covid-19 rules are strictly enforced. Our bags were scanned; we were swiped with metal detectors and were checked into the departure lounge. Within a few minutes, our flight was announced, and we boarded.

The interior of the plane was cool and beautiful. Kelvin had the window seat, and we were set to enjoy the one-hour flight. Just as I marvelled at how our travel time could not be compared to travelling by road, the plane speakers came on and the flight crew welcomed us on board. They went through the routine of safety while aboard, and what should be done in the case of an emergency landing. I wanted to listen, but Kelvin did not seem interested.

'It's just a one-hour flight, Riche,' he said. But I listened anyway.

'What people can achieve,' he said.

'What? What did you say?' I asked.

'Oh!' he said. 'I was just thinking about what we could achieve as human beings. How our lives could be so much amazing if we channelled our energies and power of imagination to the right things.'

'Hmm,' I said.

'Hmm' was an expression of disinterest from my childhood, especially if I did not add anything after it. If the speaker did not get the cue and continued speaking, I would torture him by answering him in monotones. I said 'Hmmn' now because I was nervous. What would I say to Ejiro when I got to Lagos? Why had she even invited me over? I'd rather talk about all these, but Kelvin wanted to talk about the possibilities of the human imagination.

The plane taxied for a few minutes starting from the right-wing, then the left, and finally lifted off. I watched through the window as the world around me became slanted and smaller. As we went up, the earth beneath us looked like a moving map, like a piece of elaborate Lego buildings come alive. The houses looked like oddly shaped boxes in various colours, while the roads looked like rumpled strips of black rope. Our plane gained altitude, and soon, there was nothing more to see than clouds – fluffy white things floating about the vast expanse of empty space. The pilot announced that we had reached cruising altitude and that we could unfasten our seatbelts. I loosened my seatbelt and thought about how small we all were, compared to the universe and its grand scheme of things.

'So,' Kelvin started again. 'I was talking about how our lives would just be easier if we could just think and dare to try new things. Just look at this giant bird flying in the sky. I don't know if anyone thought this would be possible two centuries ago, but we are doing it now. And we don't even know what the future holds, what we can do if we think! Maybe we can slip through time to the future or go back to the past.'

My mind drifted. I knew how Kelvin's thoughts could run wide when he was taken in with an idea. But I was more concerned with the immediate questions at hand. What does Ejiro want? What do I want with her? What do I hope for? I prayed fervently that our time apart would not affect our interaction. I hoped that my job situation would not make me ashamed. I must have dozed off at some point as these thoughts ran through my mind because an air hostess tapped me lightly.

'Please, fasten your seatbelt, sir. The pilot has announced descent.'

I looked at her and read her name tag - Caroline. It was written in red across a white plastic badge. It matched her red lipstick and stood out against her off-white shirt. I murmured my thanks. She motioned me to an in-flight food pack on a tray in front of me and asked me to hold it and fold the tray back. I did. Kelvin looked at me and smiled. Caroline disappeared.

The pilot began to descend, and the city of Lagos came into view.

The first thing I noticed about the city was that it hardly contained any green spaces; it was mostly concrete, steel and dust. Lagos looked like a factory with many moving parts from above, but I knew it would be better on the ground. The slanted view came into focus, then a bump. We had landed. The airport buildings rushed past us as the plane taxied to a stop.

The pilot bid us welcome to Lagos, thanked us for flying with the airline, and said he hoped to see us on another flight soon. The aeroplane doors opened, and everyone started moving to the exit. Kelvin and I sat and waited till the plane had almost emptied out, then we made our way out. Lagos is a city of paradoxes. Squalor exists side by side with grand opulence. Big, beautiful, and expensive space opens to admit the upper crust of society while their gates swarm with beggars like tourists drawn to a national monument. Robberies occur in broad daylight, and obscene profanities sometimes happen in places of worship. Lagos is never quiet. The streets are busy by day and lit at night. The streetlights served to show fair-skinned or dark-skinned girls of all sizes – traders in the flesh, who were reputed to give all kinds of pleasure for a fee.

Out of the plane and in the airport terminal, Kelvin called an Uber, and we were soon on our way into the city. Our first stop was at a mall. I needed to pick up a gift for Ejiro. I had often heard of the City Mall at Ikeja, that it was a beautiful place with many stores. When we got there, I saw that there were also people who didn't come to buy anything or people who came to buy things they could get in a shop on their street. These were people who came for the shopping experience and the feeling of worth which the spaces conferred on its patrons. Kelvin insisted that I buy a pair of jeans and two tee-shirts for myself.

After the mall, the cab dropped us at a hotel in Maryland where

Kelvin had a brief meeting. I stayed at the hotel restaurant to eat and watch a football game until Kelvin came to get me an hour later, and we were off to Ejiro's house. Another Uber and another driver. Mr new driver was chatty and wanted to educate us on the dynamics of driving an Uber. I was bored and uninterested, but Kelvin was all ears. I had a feeling that he wanted a basis for comparison or hoped to get something that he could take back to Sierra Leone. I was right. Kelvin asked many questions, so many that the Uber driver became uncomfortable and asked him if he was a quality control officer from Uber. Kelvin replied that he was not; he was a visitor to Nigeria. The Uber driver was silent for a while, but his propensity soon got the better of him and he resumed talking with gusto.

'This Uber work wey we dey do, na only Uber dey gain inside o. Imagine, na twenty-five per cent dem dey collect. I go buy fuel, maintain my moto. Wetin remain?'

We were both silent and let him talk. I looked at the pin on the Google Map; we were almost at Ejiro's house. On the street, a child beggar was pursuing a Lexus SUV and begging for alms. A woman selling bottled water ran after a bus to collect her money after giving water to a passenger. A bus conductor cursed at a traffic light, and I saw four LASTMA officials arrest a Keke Napep, which, according to them, the state government just disbanded from Lagos.

The minute we drove into GRA, Ikeja, there was a noticeable difference. Tall fences topped with barbed wires shielded even taller houses. Everything was neat and prim; the traffic light actually worked. Our Google Map pin turned when we got to a black gate. A voice on the driver's phone informed us that we had reached our destination. As if for effect, our driver turned as the car idled, 'You are welcome, sir,' he said. 'Na de place be this.'

Ejiro's house was a massive black gate and a tall concrete fence spilling over with Angelonia flowers. The flowers outside the fence bore testimony to the work of a master horticulturist. One of the flowers was treated and shaped like a horse standing on its legs; others were shaped after different images.

'Honk,' Kelvin told the Uber driver.

A dog barked. The driver honked again, and a pedestrian gate opened. A very dark man in what must have once been a white babariga came out. His clothes had definitely seen better days, but he looked well-fed. He came to the car.

'Good eebnig, Oga,' he said.

'Hello. Good evening.'

'Abeg, oga, who I dey pine?'

'I am looking for Ejiro.'

Kelvin shifted beside me, perhaps not used to sitting in a car answering to security men at the gate.

'Ejiro? No pe here.'

'She gave me this address.'

I handed him the paper. He took it and scanned it.

'Toh, who you be? Who make e say I dey pine am?'

'Tell am say Richard.'

'Oga, no pes, make e go tell am. I dey come.'

Kelvin and I sat in the car and waited. I quickly took a look at my clothes and the gifts I brought for Ejiro. I caught Kelvin's face in the rear-view mirror and saw that he had a smirk on his face.

'Richard, you really want this thing to happen,' he said.

I laughed uneasily.

The maiguard opened the gate and asked us to come in. We drove in and he opened the car door for Kelvin, running around to open my door.

'Oga, barka dai zuwa. I no know say I be anti priend.'

'No sweat, you are just doing your job,' Kelvin responded and gave the maiguard one thousand Naira.

'Ah, Oga? God pless you flenty flenty.'

Ejiro finally got to the car. 'Hi, Richard. I am so glad you could come.'

'Thank you, Ejiro. Thank you for inviting me.'

'And you brought company,' she observed.

'Erm, Ejiro, this is Kelvin, my friend from university. We came together, but he is also in Lagos for business. Kelvin is a man's man, if you know what I mean.'

Kelvin bowed good-naturedly and Ejiro smiled. Once the light came into her eyes, she transformed and became more beautiful. Ejiro's smile revealed sparkling white teeth and dimples on each cheek.

'Is that how we will be doing formal-formal in my house abi? Come here.'

She drew me into a hug that lasted close to a minute. She then beckoned towards the house.

'Come in, please,' she said and led the way into the building.

I looked at the compound. It was huge and had open spaces playing hosts to various plants. I could recognise at least four Jacaranda, Morning Glory, Ixora, and Frangipani. I wondered what effort it took to maintain such beauty amidst Lagos' dust and noise.

Then, there was the house. It was magnificent and painted in bright colours. I wondered how much tears, sweat, and blood it took to build such an imposing structure. What did it take for a young man to succeed? An inadequate and outmoded education like the ones currently given in our higher institutions, or diminishing opportunities like the one I presently sought at Supreme Oil?

I put the thoughts aside as I stepped into Ejiro's house. Tonight was about rekindling an old flame. Who knew what fire could start if the visit was handled right?

'What are you thinking about?' Ejiro broke into my thoughts.

'Hmmn.'

'I said, what are you thinking about? You were practically gone.' Ejiro smiled, and it lit up her eyes and accentuated her dimples.

'Oh, I was just marvelling at this magnificent house.'

'Oh, you'll soon get used to it. My father says it all the time that this is his most solid investment, so he put a lot into it.'

The grandeur of the house did not diminish on the inside. In the sitting room, muted lights gave the place a cosy feeling. The ambience was of a place where intimate and serious discussions could be had and not a word of it would reach the ears of the world. It felt like a grove of secrets. I wondered what memories had been made here.

Ejiro pointed at an exquisite chandelier hanging from the hollow ceiling. 'My father had that custom-made in China.'

'Wow,' I said. My 'wow' collided with Kelvin's comment.

'It's beautiful.'

'You're welcome, guys. Come, let's eat. You must be starving.' Ejiro pointed to the dining area.

The dining area was separated from the main sitting room by a steel balcony. There was a big oak table surrounded by eight straight-backed chairs, all sitting on a raised platform. The dining area was decorated with a smaller but still exquisite chandelier, oozing warm lights. The meal was a two-course affair of rice, fried plantains, and vegetables, to be washed down with some wine and, later, pepper soup. Ejiro turned to Kelvin and said she hoped his palate was suited for Nigerian cuisine. Kelvin laughed and told her in pidgin that he had eaten Nigerian food for five years and could do it any time of day or night.

After dinner, Ejiro's sister, Blessing, joined us. She and Kelvin soon discovered their mutual interest in football and were arguing when Ejiro and I slipped away. We found our way to some garden chairs under the stars. I was thinking about how I was going to start a conversation. On her part, Ejiro seemed to be basking in the evening breeze, with the fragrance of flowers around. There had to be a rose bush somewhere because its scent wafted in, on the evening breeze.

Ejiro waited for me to speak. Although I could be described as a talkative when I'm with close friends, starting a conversation with Ejiro became hard. Shyness and paradoxical exhilaration constituted the reason for my instant, yet temporary, stammering.

'Ejiro, I...'

'Why did you come here?' Ejiro asked.

'Excuse me?' I said.

'I said, why did you come?'

I was shocked by this question. But I quickly composed myself. 'Ejiro, you invited me,' I reminded her.

'Yes, I know. But why did you come? PH is a long way from here, and you could have chosen not to come.'

There are times when a question is a snare; whatever answer one gives would land one in a hot sticky mess. Not answering at all showed cowardice and weakness, especially when one could not discern the question's intentions. I did not know Ejiro's intention. And I quickly recalled our phone conversations to see if I had said anything wrong or untoward. I could not remember. So, I decided to brave through Ejiro's question with braggadocio.

'Ejiro, what do you want? You invited me here all the way from Port Harcourt and I honoured your invitation. Thank you for asking me here; thank you for the food. Perhaps, it's time for me to leave.' I made to stand up.

'Richard, please.' Ejiro's left hand had gripped my right hand. 'I am sorry I left the way I did. But we were young and I did not have the latitude I have now. There really was nothing I could have done. In fact, I have done nothing with my love for you. My feelings for you are still intact.'

I sat quietly. Perhaps she would say more. She didn't, so I volunteered, 'Ejiro, I wrote you letters. I don't know how many letters I wrote. You never replied even one.'

'I did not get your letters, Richard. Not one. My father intercepted them all. I did not know until I stumbled on them one day. Your letters and mine.'

I sighed.

'Richard, even though I was uncertain, I did not lose my love for you. You are my first love, and I have never forgotten you.'

'Ejiro, time has passed. It's been quite a while since we last thought of each other like this. But Ejiro, I have not lost my love for you. Seeing you again made me realise you are the one I have been searching for all my life; that I have been comparing every other person to you.'

'What are you saying, Richard?'

'I have missed you, Ejiro. But it can't be like old times. I have grown; I have experienced life and seen places. I have the weight of experience in my life now and I understand more. So, I can't offer you the rash thoughtlessness of our teenage years. I have outgrown that. All I have to give is mature love. Do you accept it?'

Ejiro looked at my face. 'Arrgh, Richard! What the heck! Do you have to make love a little lecture?'

'Actually, I do not. But I have to know what it is you really want from me. So, what do you want, Ejiro?'

'What I really want? I--,' she trailed off and leaned into my face.

Before I could think, we were kissing. It was passionate and signalled old times accompanied by an urge from a million years ago. We held ourselves close, staring at each other's eyes even as the soft kiss and simultaneous embrace continued. I really can't tell how much time passed or what moved around us. However, I know that our flames of passion were yet to quench. We were still in that very emotional mood when somebody coughed and we sprang apart. Blessing was standing by the garden chairs.

'Sorry to bother you, but I think your friend has been looking for you.'

'Oh,' I said. 'Yes, Kelvin.'

I looked at Blessing's face and tried to smile; she smiled back.

'I'll go tell him that you are on your way,' Blessing said, pointing to the direction of the house.

As soon as Blessing left, I turned to Ejiro to say something.

'Shhh,' she said, putting her index finger on my lips. 'Don't worry about Blessing; she is cool. Plus, mum and dad are in the US.'

'Okay, let's go,' I said.

'Just a little bit more,' Ejiro said, pecking me some more. 'Next time, come alone.'

'Okay,' I said. I quickly arranged my features while she didn't seem to bother with hers. 'Let's go.'

An Uber had arrived to take Kelvin and me to our hotel in less than fifteen minutes. I waved to Ejiro and Blessing and promised to call every day. Ejiro also told me that she would be in Port Harcourt in a fortnight, and I was already looking forward to it. Ejiro pecked me on the cheek again, and our driver drove into the night.

Our car had hardly left Ejiro's house when Kelvin turned to me and said, 'So, tell me all about it.'

'About what?' I asked.

'Hey, Richard, don't play with me. You and that girl went away for so long in the dark, and now you are bullshitting me? Do you even know how you looked when you came back and how your voice sounded husky? You better start talking. I want to hear everything.'

Kelvin was not so easily deterred. Also, I knew that he meant well. So, I told him about our discussion and how the flames of our passion were kindled under the stars, and how his 'acolyte' had come to interrupt us.

Kelvin laughed at my use of the word.

'Richard, that girl is not likely to be anybody's acolyte. And she definitely knows her sister more than you are giving her credit for. When she came back from you guys, she had a smirk on her face. "They will be here soon if they don't bite each other's tongue off", she said. I knew something interesting was up.'

I smiled sheepishly.

'So, Riche, what are your plans for this girl?'

'I love that girl, Kelvin. I have loved her for a long time. I'll take things one day at a time.'

By the time we got back to the hotel, it was a few minutes past midnight. Kelvin set the alarm for 5 a.m. He had one last meeting with some steel magnates before our afternoon flight at 1 p.m.

I knew what the next day would be like. Kelvin would go for his business meeting while I would spend my day availing myself of the hotel's excellent room service. Ejiro would come and we would spend some time together before Kelvin returned, and we had to leave for Port Harcourt. We would not take an Uber; instead, Ejiro would take us to the airport in one of their family cars. Kelvin would step down while Ejiro and I would share a brief, passionate kiss. We would make promises to each other to call every day. Kelvin and I would go into the womb of the plane and Ejiro would go back home.

But our relationship, unlike matter, may not have physical weight, but it would occupy space – the whole stretch of cyberspace from Lagos to Port Harcourt.

At about 3 p.m., the pilot announced that we had entered the Port Harcourt airspace. He announced the weather condition and commenced descent. From above, the city looked like a factory with moving parts. But these factories contained many bodies of water. The mist cleared, and the city came into focus. Port Harcourt was enveloped by the dour colours of evening and grey tint of soot, and small packets of light punctuated it.

We touched down. Once we got down from the plane, Kelvin called his taxi driver on the phone, and he came in about ten minutes. We would go to my house first, then the taxi would take Kelvin back to his hotel.

The traffic crawled because of the closing hour crowd. People were just returning from work.

'The closer you are to God, the less time you get to spend on small things,' Kelvin said.

I smiled, but I wasn't listening. I was looking out for bole and fish. I sighted some hawkers at Omagwa Junction, near the airport. All of them were jostling to sell things. But there was this girl who seemed like she was keen to observe the cars and faces of people on the road. Occasionally, she ran after a car or two, then she came back to her spot and continued to observe them.

'Kelvin, look at that girl. Is she serious at all? It is like she has her own customers, and she is waiting for them.'

'Richard, that girl may be tired or something. And perhaps, looking at cars maybe her favourite past-time. She looks nice, though; almost refined.'

'I hear you. But something is off about this girl. She is not keen enough for Port Harcourt traffic sales. I am sure she is new. But not to worry, she will soon learn.'

Kelvin did not comment. After a few seconds, he continued his former chit-chat. 'Look, Riche, God is in heaven, abi? So being up there in the plane, we were so close to Him, and there was no traffic. Now, look at us, on the ground. See this traffic, go slow.'

I smiled again. Kelvin had a way of blending humour with what some people might consider sublime wisdom. I started to think about it, too. What if we had travelled by road? Would we have come back in one piece? Could our car not have broken down because of bad roads? Perhaps we could have been robbed or molested by gun-toting policemen on the highway. There was no difference between policemen and thieves on the highway. They all extort money from travellers at gunpoint. They would have stopped us and demanded our phones, maybe forced us to open our phones' security codes and search every single app. They would check, ranging from Facebook to Google Hangout to Instagram and every single email on the phone. They would have embarrassed us and called us 'Yahoo boys,' extorting a huge amount of money from us. The police preferred to check the phones of young men to extort them than to carry out genuine operations to fight crime. Herdsmen or bandits would have kidnapped us etc.

I have heard many complaints from friends and even on social media where police demand to check the phones of any young man driving an exotic car. The police, however, do not do that to prosecute these people they tagged as internet fraudsters, but to extort money from them; hence, scamming the scammers. Before we travelled to Lagos, there was a nationwide protest against the Special Anti-Robbery Squad (SARS) (#EndSars) for extortion and extra-judicial killings. If the Inspector General of Police had not quickly moved to discipline the officers involved and restructured the unit, we would not have escaped police extortion and brutality, especially by the rank and files stationed on highways.

'Kelvin made us escape such legitimate harassment and stress,' I reasoned.

'We are here,' Kelvin said, breaking into my thoughts.

'Thank you, Kelvin. We'll talk on the phone.'

'Yes,' Kelvin said and waved. The car zoomed off.

Home sweet home. I walked into the compound, hoping to find Nelly. How had he fared in my absence?

Chapter 5

MONDAY mornings are the busiest mornings of the week. Busy because Mondays are designed to be like that because of perception; busy because everyone has had the chance to rest and recharge their batteries. I once read on Facebook that the best cure for insomnia is a Monday morning. I wasn't exactly sure what it meant.

I did not have anywhere to be until Tuesday. So, I figured I could just laze around a bit, go to see Kelvin in the afternoon, and prepare for my interview the next day. I was just thinking about breakfast when my phone rang. It was Ejiro.

'Hello, Ejiro. How are you, darling?'

Silence.

'Hello, hello. Oh, this damned network!'

'It's not the network. I can hear you loud and clear,' Ejiro said on the other end.

'Oh,' I smiled. 'Hello, Ejiro, how are you, my darling?'

'I'm not sure.'

'You are not sure? What's the matter? Is anything wrong?'

'Yes, Richard. You are the matter.'

'Err, I don't understand.'

'Why didn't you call me when you got to Port Harcourt? I took you to the airport, and you couldn't even call me to let me know you had landed. What if something had happened? How would I know?

You just left me hanging here, making me listen to the news to see if there was a crash or something. I even thought maybe somebody stole your phone.'

I knew from experience not to intrude when Ejiro had these outbursts. It was amusing, but I dared not laugh.

'You say you love me, and you couldn't even call me after you have been on a journey. How will I know you arrived safely? How will I know that all is well? How will I--'

'Hello, how will I know not to worry when you... Wait, Richard, are you there? You are not saying anything!'

'Hello,' I stood up from the settee and walked back to my room for privacy. 'Hello, Ejiro. Darling, I am sorry. I forgot. Kelvin and I had so much to do when we got back. I did not have the presence of mind to call you.'

'Ah, Richard, and you said you love me?'

'I do, baby. Omalicha nwa, my sunshine. Ndo, I won't do that again.'

'You better don't do that again.'

Laughter had come into her voice, making me exhale too.

'So, how are you this morning?' I asked.

'Now that I heard your voice, I feel better.'

I laughed. 'I am sorry I made you feel bad. It wasn't intentional. Please forgive me.'

'So, going out today?'

'Yes,' I answered. 'I have to prepare for an outing tomorrow and meet up with Kelvin.'

'Okay, but call me in the evening, ehn?'

'I will, love,' I said.

'Thank you, love. I love you.'

'Love you too, darling.'

I put the phone down and noticed that its notification light was blinking. I picked it again and saw an SMS from Supreme Oil and Gas HR. It read:

> *Dear Richard C,*
> *Please be informed that your interview with us has been rescheduled from Wednesday, October 16th to Tuesday, October 15th at 9 am. Please be prompt and prepare for a full day.*
> *Yours, Supreme HR.*

This text excited and scared me. Why was the interview rescheduled? Was I being considered above other people for the position? Why was I asked to prepare for a full day? Was there going to be a crowd? If there was a crowd, would I get the job? Tomorrow? Was I prepared? Why so early? 9 am. What if I was caught in traffic? Do I have the right kind of clothes? What would I do? If I appeared shabby, would I look desperate? If I looked desperate, would they offer me low pay? What if they asked me who referred me? Would we go on to have a lifeless conversation about irrelevant things, or would they find me worthy of engagement even though I knew no one?

All my questions seemed to lead me to a dead end. I decided that I would go and see it to the end. No man has ever won something he did not risk; no one ever got celebrated for a risk he did not take. I would go. It had not even been a question if I was going or not. The real thing was that I would go and would not stop putting in my best until the last word was said. First, I needed to eat; then, I needed to step out to get a few things.

I couldn't eat breakfast eventually. Anxiety had done something to my appetite. I decided to head out. I wanted to see Kelvin and ask him what I should expect since he knew the people at Supreme Oil and Gas. I also wanted him to help me pick out a suit. After that, I would head back home and get some rest and prepare for the interview.

I hailed a cab and gave him the directions to Kelvin's hotel. We were soon on the move. The traffic was true to its spirit. Everyone went out on Mondays and it meant that traffic often crawled in the city. As we drove on, I mused at the reason I had been unable to call Ejiro when we arrived.

Our front door was locked when Kelvin dropped me off at home. I quickly opened the door and stepped in. It was comforting that the house had been cleaned, and everything seemed in order until I entered Nelly's room. It was a mess. It was unusual for him to leave anything out of its place, so I became agitated. What had happened in my absence? Had Nelly's sorrow got the better of him and made him hurt himself? Where was he? No sooner had these thoughts entered my mind; I started to panic and called Nelly's number. I tried his two lines, and they rang through. I called a few of his friends, but he wasn't with them. Then I called Aunty Rose. Her line rang out too. I did not know what to do, so I waited. Aunty Rose called back after twenty-five minutes. What was the matter? She wanted to know. I asked if she had seen Nelly. She replied she had seen him on Friday evening at the close of work and wanted to know if everything was all right. I told her I had just returned from a trip and did not meet Nelly at home. Eventually, sleep won the battle against worry, and I slept off on the couch.

The sound of someone hitting the door woke me. When I checked the time, it was a few minutes to 11 p.m. Who could it be? Then I remembered that I had not seen my brother since I came back from Lagos. Perhaps it was him. I went quickly to the door and opened it. There stood Nelly, reeking of alcohol.

'Nelly, what happened?' I asked, trying to not raise my voice.

Instead of answering, Nelly ran inside and went straight to the toilet. As I looked outside to see if anyone had followed him home, I heard him puke, then the sound of the water closet flushing. Nelly came out of the toilet and went to his room. By the time I pulled myself together to ask what happened to him, he had fallen asleep. I made my way to my room too, said a short prayer on my bed, and drifted off to sleep. Things got better in the morning. Nelly woke up early and was not hungover. He took care of his room and went to work.

I arrived at Kelvin's hotel room while he was getting set to have breakfast. My stomach suddenly discovered its appetite and began to growl. But it shouldn't have worried because Kelvin was already calling the reception to make his order a double and have it brought up to his room quickly.

'I wasn't really expecting you here today,' Kelvin said. 'I thought you'd be resting after all that travel.'

'Yes, Kelvin. I was going to rest until I got this.'

I gave him my phone with the text message. He read it and looked up.

'Wow, they moved your interview down?'

'They did. All that wanting to rest cleared from my eyes. I came to ask for your help. What should I expect?'

'Oh, nothing really unusual. Obviously, you passed the written test; that's why you were invited for this second stage interview. They would want to see that you know what you are doing and that you have the technical know-how for the position you applied for. Beyond that, they'll want to see that you have the ethics required to work in a company of that magnitude and that you can survive under the kind of pressure they constantly have to deal with.'

I was silent.

'So, beyond knowledge, they may deliberately create difficult situations for you, and you won't even know that you are being role-played. When you get there, keep your cool. There was this time a guy attended an interview. He arrived very early, was properly dressed and sat at the reception. They had sent a message that the interview would start at 9.30 am. He waited patiently until the time of the interview. Unfortunately, the interview did not start at the proposed time. He and three other people were there in the room for another hour. While the time passed, he complained to the lady beside him, who gave him complete attention and even slipped a few anecdotes. From complaining, he went on to divulge personal information about himself and the company he worked for before. There was another lady and a man there. The other lady tried to make small talk with the other man, but he was simply polite and said nothing else. He did not complain; neither was he irritable. After an hour had passed, the two women excused themselves. The talkative man was called in. To cut a long story short, our friend, the talkative, did not get the job. The woman he was complaining to, was on the panel of interviewers, and they had come to test the two leading candidates for work ethics.'

'So, he lost the job because he talked too much?'

'Yes, that's exactly what I am saying.'

Our breakfast arrived while Kelvin was telling this story. Kelvin nodded his thanks, and the waiter quietly left the room.

Chapter 6

NELLY got home early and full of smiles. Kelvin and I had just returned from the boutique where he had escorted me to pick a suit for my interview. He had no meeting and was not in a hurry. As he told me about the success of his trip and his plan to return home at the end of the week, Nelly bustled in.

'Have you guys heard the news?' he said without greeting.

'Good evening, Nell,' I said.

'What news?' Kelvin said, ignoring my jibe at Nelly.

'Aunty Rose has just been appointed to the Court of Appeal in Lagos!'

'Really?' I said. 'That calls for a great celebration. We should visit.'

'Who will be overseeing her practice here in Port Harcourt?' Kelvin asked.

'That is the good part. Guess who is going to be overseeing the day-to-day running of the chamber?' Nelly said.

I looked at Nelly. 'No way!'

'Yes way,' he said.

'No way,' I said again.

'Yes way,' Nelly said. 'The new Head of Legal Operations at Rosie Scott is yours truly.'

'OMG! Wow! Congrats, Nelly.'

'Well done, Nelly,' Kelvin said, enthused.

Nelly bowed good-naturedly. 'Thank you,' he said. 'So, what're all these?' Nelly gestured at the suit and shoes. 'Somebody getting married?'

'Actually, no. Somebody is trying to get a job at Supreme Oil and Gas,' Kelvin said.

'Wonderful. So, this is an interview then?'

'Yes, first thing tomorrow.'

'I am glad. Good luck, bro.'

'Thanks, man. And congratulations again.'

'Thank you. I need to get this shirt off.'

Nelly went in to remove his clothes and soon came back wearing blue cotton shorts and a grey tee-shirt. We sat before the television, scanning the stations. I liked the picture that we formed: three young men enjoying each other's company and looking forward to success. I was contemplating this picture when Kelvin's phone rang.

'I need to take this. It's Juliet,' Kelvin stood and stepped into my room. He was there a while, and I decided to talk to Nelly about Ejiro.

'Nelly, do you remember Ejiro?'

'The one you told me you met recently?'

I nodded.

'What about her?'

'How do you like her for a sister-in-law?'

Nelly paused briefly. 'Indifferent.'

'What do you mean by indifferent?'

'I don't mean she is not a good person. I am just wondering that you guys just reconnected after almost ten years.'

'Okay.'

'Don't you think it's rather too fast? I would have thought you'd get to know each other all over again, see how you have both changed and see if you can work things out. This in-law thing is too sudden, abeg. I mean, it's been what, two to three weeks?'

Thank you, Nelly. I get your meaning. I am not saying I am marrying now. I'm just asking what you think about her, that's all.'

Okay, then. Sorry. The prospects do not look bad.'

'Hey, what prospects are you guys talking about? You people are talking business behind my back?' Kelvin challenged as he made his way back to the living room.

'Ah, Kelvin, which business again?' I said.

'Don't mind him, Kelvin. He is talking about Ejiro's business.'

'Right. Ministry of Women Affairs.'

We all laughed.

'So, have you guys spoken today?' Kelvin wanted to know.

I made a face.

'Hmmn, Kelvin, you are asking? Who did you think big brother here was talking to on the phone before yours truly got out of bed?'

Kelvin and Nelly laughed again; I did not join.

'Yours truly needs to go now. Riche, good luck tomorrow. Let me know when you are done. Don't forget the things we talked about,' Kelvin said to me.

'I won't,' I said.

'Thank you for coming, Kelvin,' Nelly said.

'The pleasure's mine,' Kelvin replied and gave a mock bow.

Kelvin had called his cab driver. He pulled in just as we stepped out of the house. We bid each other goodnight. Kelvin's cab drove into the darkening night, and I returned to the familiarity of our apartment.

I arrived at Supreme Oil and Gas at about 8:30 a.m. The gateman wanted to know why I was there.

'Good morning. How may I help you, please?'

'Good morning, sir. I am here for an interview.'

'You are welcome. Can I see your invite, please?'

'Yes.' I presented my phone with the text message sent to me on the screen.

The security officer took a look at it and asked, 'What is your name, please?'

'Richard Chukwu,' I said.

He checked for my name against a list on his computer.

'You are welcome, sir. Please, go straight and turn left.' He pointed as he described the place. 'You are going to the administrative block. It's the first building after you turn.'

He handed me a tag; it read 'Visitor'. 'Please put this around your neck.'

'Thank you,' I said, taking the tag and wearing it.

I went in the direction the security officer indicated. As I walked, I look around the surroundings of Supreme Oil. The premises were large and impressive. The company had several buildings, and each was as big as a full-fledged mansion. In front of each building was a façade that indicated what section of Supreme Oil the building housed. I saw Engineering and Technical; Business Development; Freight and Off-shore; CSR; Administrative and others. I noticed that the buildings, though the same size, had a distinct look to each one. Engineering had a factory-like look, and the few people I saw around it were in helmets and coveralls. I could tell at a glance that the people in Technical were electrical people who dealt with light and gas. CSR, Business and Administration looked similar. I imagined that the duties in these three departments may sometimes overlap. These three areas contained the prim and well-dressed people who ensured that all aspects of the company worked like a well-oiled engine.

I got to the building marked 'Administration', took a deep breath and walked in. Once in, I found myself in a large reception. The area was all glass, gloss and shine. The people here carried themselves with a kind of importance like they realised that they were the company's gatekeepers.

I approached the counter and told the personnel there that I had come for an interview. Politely, they directed me to a waiting area and asked me to join the people I met there. We would be called in one by one.

Aunty Rose was moving to Lagos. Since her appointment to the Court of Appeal, visitors poured into her house and office to congratulate her and make themselves known. A part of me jokingly wondered if these people planned to get into trouble and thought their friendship with an Appeal Court judge would come in handy.

We arrived at Aunty Rose's house around 5:30 in the evening. Kelvin had decided to accompany Nelly and I to congratulate Aunty Rose and bid her farewell. When we got there, Uncle Scott was playing the gracious host. I thought it was good of him to celebrate his wife for this landmark achievement. When Kelvin and I talked about it, he said it was because the man was European. Most African men, Kelvin had opined, had a gene that made them feel threatened by a woman's success. We all laughed, but Kelvin was serious. He added that it did not matter who that woman was. Nelly asked Kelvin if he was that kind of man. Kelvin replied that he was of that percentage outside the most. I wondered if I was that kind of man too, seeing that I was dating a woman whose parents were richer than my family.

'Hello, mate,' Uncle Scott called from across the room. 'How are you? I am glad to see you.'

'Good evening, Uncle Scott. I'm doing great. Thank you,' I replied. 'This is Kelvin, my friend.'

Uncle Scott had insisted Nelly and me call him by his first name, and he would cringe whenever we addressed him as 'Uncle'. But he had gotten used to it when after several attempts to stop us, we were never able to remove the 'African' in us. Aunty Rose had eventually taken the time to explain the Nigerian culture of respect for others, especially for people older, and Uncle Scott had lost his sensitivity to 'Uncle'. I could even say he had begun to enjoy the sound of it.

'Hello, Kelvin. How do you do?'

'How do you do too?' Kelvin replied.

I was admiring a new figurine when Aunty Rose came in.

'Ah, my babies are finally here. Hello, lovelies. How are you?'

'Fine ma,' I replied for everyone.

'I hope you boys haven't had lunch.'

'No,' Kelvin laughed. 'We were hoping we'd get some lunch and dinner here.'

'Great! That's what I want to hear. Come to the table.'

'And you,' she pointed to Nelly. 'Stop being so uptight. We are no longer in the office. I am not your boss here at home; I am your beloved aunt.'

Nelly nodded and smiled.

'Let's eat,' Aunty Rose said.

The food was an elaborate two-course affair of pounded yam with egusi soup, with hot pepper soup served first as an appetiser. Each course was accompanied with huge chunks of meat.

'Aunty, I'll be returning to Sierra Leone this weekend,' Kelvin informed Aunty Rose.

She looked up from her food. 'You will? You are tired of us already?'

'No, ma. I love Nigeria, but I have to go home. I am most grateful for the time I have spent here. My business pursuits have met with huge success. It's time to go home and finish up some contracts.'

'Well, it is good. But we have gotten used to you. I was hoping you'll let us get you a nice Nigerian girl.'

Kelvin laughed. 'I have really enjoyed my time here. About the Nigerian girl, I will have to think about it. But my greatest joy is that I found this one,' he pointed at me, 'after all these years.'

I gave a mock bow on my seat, then said, 'I have news too. I have been offered a position at Supreme Oil and Gas as an Assistant Supervisor in the technical department. I am to pick up my appointment letter tomorrow.'

'What?' Nelly exclaimed.

'Great news,' Kelvin said. 'Why did you keep this a secret?'

'I wanted it to be a surprise,' I said. 'Actually, the call came today.'

Aunty Rose was enthused. She came around the table and hugged me. 'Congratulations, my baby. I am proud of you. Your persistence has finally paid off.'

'Thank you, Aunty.'

Aunty Rose returned to her seat and proposed a toast. She was thankful for all the good things that were happening. I had gotten a job; Kelvin had done well in business; Nelly was now Head of Operations at her chambers, and she was going to Lagos on a national assignment. She raised her glass.

'To better days.'

'To better days,' we all repeated.

We clinked glasses and drank our wine.

Kelvin had one more night to spend in Nigeria. Things had gone incredibly well. He invited Nelly and me out to celebrate with him. We agreed to meet at Sky Bar, one of the best restaurants in Port Harcourt, on the third floor of the Genesis Centre, located on Tombia Street. Sky Bar was one of those places I had fantasised about. I had hoped that one day, the work of my hands would be enough to make me walk into that restaurant as a customer and order food without fear. It turned out that friendship and loyalty had carried me thus far. I was grateful for my friendship with Kelvin.

Nelly and I left the house at about 5:30 p.m. I had just returned from collecting my appointment letter, and Nelly had returned from his new position as Head of Operations at Aunty Rose's chambers. She took him through the workings of running the firm and making sure that he got his structures in place. Though Nelly was the head and he had experienced people working with him, he still had to report to Aunty Rose. However, all this could not be done publicly because Aunty Rose was now in the public eye.

I was enthused about my prospect of starting work on Monday, but I was also careful because I did not know the kind of people I would be working with. However, I knew that hard work and competence always spoke for themselves and earned respect for the doer. As we got into the car, I started to tell Nelly about the part Kelvin had played in getting me the job. Unknown to me, before going for the interview, Kelvin had pulled a few strings and informed the people at Supreme Oil and Gas that I was his friend. He had given me such glowing tributes that the interviewers were willing to give me a chance to prove myself.

When I went to pick up my letter, the human resources manager directed me to the MD's office.

'Good morning, sir,' I said as I entered the expansive office.

He waved me to a seat. I sat. The MD closed the files he was working on and looked me straight in the eyes. I blinked and lowered my gaze.

'Welcome to Supreme Oil and Gas,' he said.

'Thank you, sir.'

'Do you know why you were chosen for this role?'

I blinked again. I did not want to risk sounding proud or unsure of myself. If I said something about being good, it might imply that I was proud and did not think that other applicants were equally good. If I sounded unsure, I could be making the MD think I was not the best fit for the job. Hubris and hamartia were so interlinked; one could not often be sure where one ended and the other began. My best bet was silence. I looked at the table.

'My young man,' the MD continued, 'there were three other first-class graduates among those of you called for the last stage of the interview. But you stood out because of your ingenuity. However, your friend Kelvin also called me on your behalf. He gave his word that you are hardworking, and he told me that you are, in fact, responsible for his academic excellence. I like that young man, and I have worked with him. I find him to be very sensible and intelligent. So, if he told me that you are part of his making, then I am interested in you.'

I looked up and smiled. 'Thank you, sir.'

'We are placing a huge trust on you as an Assistant Supervisor in the technical unit. I hope you won't betray this trust. I hope you won't let us down, and your friend, too.'

'I won't, sir.'

'Good. This is your letter. I wanted to give it to you personally because of my relationship with Kelvin. I wish you a good time here, and I hope you will do a good job.'

'I will, sir. I promise. Thank you.'

'All right, then,' the MD stood up. 'Welcome to Supreme.'

'Thank you, sir,' I said.

Nelly was surprised when I finished my story. 'You should really thank Kelvin when we get there. I think we should stop and buy him a gift.'

'We are late, but we can get him one on our way home. I can give it to him at the airport. His flight is an evening flight.'

'Okay.'

'We are here,' the driver said and pulled into Genesis. We got off, paid the taxi driver and made our way into the restaurant.

Amidst chilled beer and steaming plates of point-and-kill catfish pepper soup, we told stories of our university days. Kelvin reminisced about the girls who threw themselves at him and the ones he sought, albeit secretly. I did not know, he said. He ensured that I did not. He knew how to put things in compartments. He laughed now. It was surprising that most of the girls who wanted him were not the ones he wanted. And the ones he wanted did not want what he was ready to give. He was a responsible married man now, with kids. I told stories too about my search for the always elusive job and the attendant disappointments. I ended up thanking Kelvin for his kindness and prayed that the blessings of God would fall on him in my near tipsy state.

That night, I spoke with Kelvin's wife. She was reverent and thanked me for my influence in making her husband a respectable man. When she asked me about my girlfriend, I laughed and said she would meet her soon.

I also had to make my peace with Juliet, Kelvin's sister. She had waited for me to make contact. She had pined for me, even. I apologised to her and explained what happened. I also congratulated her on her engagement and her forthcoming wedding. We chatted for a while and ended the call.

Nelly and I returned home that night after I promised Kelvin that I would accompany him to the airport.

I received an urgent summon from my aunt and her husband. I left home immediately and arrived a few minutes to nine. To my greatest astonishment, they handed over the keys to one of their cars to me. They would be relocating to Lagos over the weekend and wanted me to have one of their cars since Aunty Rose would be getting an official car with her appointment. I wanted to thank them, but I could not utter a word. My mouth hung open, and tears rolled from my eyes like a ball descending from a high sloppy mountain. It wasn't until Uncle Scott asked me if I had a valid driver's licence that I recovered. Instead of answering, I smiled through my tears and offered yet my profound thanks.

My aunt handed over the papers of the car. It was a grey and full specs 2020 Ford Coupe. She asked me to maintain it well and make sure that I serviced it regularly. She also showed me all its security features and told me to ensure all the papers were renewed as and when due. After that, she offered me breakfast before I left.

Before I got to the hotel, Kelvin had called his cabman. When

I told him about the car, he paid the taxi driver a generous amount. He had planned to pay the driver off since he was leaving town, so we went to the airport in my new car.

I gave Kelvin the wristwatch I bought for him that morning. I stopped at a mall after I left my aunt's house in my car. It took about one hour before I could make up my mind on what to buy for Kelvin. The wristwatch stood out to me in the store. It was a luxury brand Versace wristwatch, and it cost me almost all the money I had in my savings, but Kelvin deserved it and much more. He was full of gratitude when I handed the gift box to him, saying he never expected to get anything from me. It was an emotional moment for both of us as we hugged when he alighted from the car. I was grateful for the gift of friendship I had with Kelvin, and I knew I was going to miss him.

As if he read my mind, he said, 'I'll miss you,' and briskly walked away.

As Kelvin went into the cool interior of the boarding gate, I thought of light. I remembered the light that streamed through the leaves on Campus Avenue the day I ran into him. First, the light had shone on Ejiro, and she and I now possessed each other. It shone on Kelvin, and he became my light to shine in the areas that I did not strike light. I had a job and I had dined in some of the places that I had only dreamt about. I remembered what they said about when light strikes water. It becomes all the colours of the rainbow, and a rainbow is a promise and a hope. Kelvin's re-entrance into my life had rekindled my hope and I planned to run really fast, to work really hard to bring my hope to fruition.

I promised myself I would see Kelvin again. I would keep in touch. The light may yet strike more water. Who knew how many more colours of the rainbow they were?

As I drove out of the airport, I made a mental note to call Ejiro and tell her the good news. But just as I joined the freeway, my phone rang. It was Ejiro.

'Hello, Richard,' Ejiro said on the other end. 'Richard, why didn't you call me since—?'

I sighted a road safety official up ahead. I did not want to risk getting pulled over on my first day of driving the car.

'Hello, Ejiro. Let me call you back in a few minutes, please. I am driving.'

'Driving?'

'Yes, baby. Driving my own car. I will tell you about it when we talk.'

'Okay. Call me o.'

'I will, dear,' I said.

Chapter 7

EJIRO screamed into my ears the moment I told her about my new job and the car. She ooh-ed and aah-ed over my aunt's appointment to the Court of Appeal and her kindness in giving me one of her cars. She was even more enthused that I had got a job in an oil company. On my part, I was happy that I now had a job and funds via my salary to take care of myself and my babe.

After she calmed down from all the screaming, Ejiro launched into a series of questions: Did I have appropriate clothes? Did the company have a dress code? Did I know if the company had a canteen? Was the food good? Could I make sure that the food did not have any contaminations before eating? What about working conditions?

I listened to all the questions, waiting to get a word in.

'Richard, why are you not answering my questions?'

'Babe, you did not let me get a word in.'

'Wait, what do you mean? Are you saying I talk too much?'

'No, o. Me! How can I say that to the love of my life?'

'Okay. Anyway, I am coming soon. Maybe this weekend.'

She sounded upbeat. Whenever Ejiro sounded upbeat, I knew something would happen. The first time I knew about this upbeat-preceding-something character was the day Kelvin and I were leaving Lagos for Port Harcourt. That morning, Kelvin had gone for his last meeting when Ejiro came in. She came in humming a love song and flipping her fingers. I had barely muttered my greetings when she kissed me softly on the lips, and soon it deepened. I responded, and our passions awoke. One by one, pieces of clothing came off, and we sought each other's bodies like people who had just survived trudging through the desert to emerge into an oasis. When my blood tipped self-found her feminine depths, it became a rhythmic ride over a smooth newfoundland. We ascended a peak of pleasure that seduced us over and over again. When we were done, it seemed as if we were both watching the world from inside a rainbow.

I was thinking to mutter my thanks, but it was she who came out with the compliment, 'You are something else. I feel like I have been attacked by a tiger.'

As I recalled this memory, I became excited. Dear God, let the weekend come now.

I resumed work on Monday. As I drove into the premises of Supreme Oil that morning, I wondered how having something to do gives one's life a semblance of purpose. What is purpose anyway? I thought a little bit about it and decided against defining it. I just knew that it felt good to wake up every morning and go to work to keep things moving in my own corner of this God's earth.

I was assigned to a temporary office at Technical and Support until my own office was completed. My office was located in a place where my supervision was needed the most. I would move in at the end of the week. Presently, my temporary office also housed three new staff, and we would be going through an orientation programme for the whole week. On the first day, we were introduced to our supervisors and instructors, who, in turn, introduced us to Supreme Oil's mode of operation. There were general modules as well as work and department-specific modules. We had to read all of these modules and submit assessments to our instructors in that first week.

The first week whirled by, and it seemed like I had gone through a single class of intensive training during that period. The first thing I noticed was that the education I received in school had done nothing to prepare me for the job I now held. What did it even mean? That I had spent so many years in school and not still be prepared to function in the industry that I longed to be in so much? What if it were up to me to set up the ground rules of operations? What would I have done with my First Class?

I was shown to my office on Friday. The walls were painted off-white and contained a swivel chair, a large desk, a settee, and a small centre table. A Supreme Oil and Gas calendar hung on the wall. The office also had a small fridge, an air conditioner, and two windows. One window looked over the technical department, and another looked out towards the quieter areas of the company.

As I settled in, a knock sounded on my door. I asked the caller to come in. When she walked in, I almost forgot to breathe. She was fair, tall, and had hair extensions up to her shoulder. She had a blue coloured top on a black skirt. Her black shoes complemented her black skirt and black hair extensions. She was beautiful to behold.

'Good morning, sir.'

'Good morning,' I said. 'Please contact the sit. What can I do for you?'

'My name is Glory Adichie, sir. I am your secretary.'

'Oh,' I said.

I remembered that I had passed through an outer office before getting into mine. I had seen that there were a desk and a chair, a fridge and a television, as well as a waiting couch. Now I knew who would sit in that office.

I took another look at Glory, and I wondered if she was also a new staff or an old hand. I hoped that her beauty was accompanied by brilliance. I decided to ask some questions.

'Thank you, err-- Can I call you Glory?'

'Yes, sir. That's what everyone calls me.' Glory smiled, revealing a set of white teeth, with a space demarcation between her top incisors.

'Okay. How long have you been working here?'

'A year and six months, sir.'

'And you've been working in this office all the time?'

'No sir,' Glory answered. 'Administrative assistants are moved around, sir. We are attached to different offices. I was rescheduled this week, and I am now to work with you.'

I asked about her qualifications and what she thought her role would be in the technical department. She responded that she was to see to the day-to-day running and administrative side of my office. She said she knew that I might require her to take care of some personal work also. I smiled and thanked her again. I told her that I hoped to keep my personal business out of the office. I told her that I would love to have a cordial relationship with everyone in the unit. She smiled and said she looked forward to that too. She returned to her office while I waited for my supervisor, who was coming to give me a final briefing and introduce me to the members of the technical department.

Soon, my mind drifted to Ejiro. She was coming this weekend, and something told me that she would make me the happiest man in the world.

Ejiro did not come that weekend. She did not come for another three weeks. When we spoke on the phone, she informed me that her parents had returned from America and she could not travel. I asked if she didn't have to come to school, but she said she had finished her course work and only came to see her research supervisor when he asked her. He hadn't called in a while, and she didn't want to come one week and have him call the next week.

Though I accepted Ejiro's excuses, I suspected there was something amiss. Every time we spoke, I sensed some tension in her voice. I asked her about it, and she laughed and asked me what the tension felt like. I laughed too. I did not want to seem possessive.

Nelly had tried of teasing me about Ejiro's postponed visits. Like me, he had settled down to work and was soon caught in the rhythms of deadlines. He often spoke in terms of court, cases, and settlements. He had Aunty Rose's support and the experience of some of her old staff. Presently, he was shopping for a legal assistant.

I had settled into my office and was, by my assessment, doing quite well. I had my subordinates' cooperation, my secretary's loyalty, and a refrigerator that was always fully stocked. The only aspect of a weekday that I did not like was when I had to drive home during the closing hour traffic.

Nelly and I were sitting in front of the TV one evening, eating dinner, when my phone rang. It was Ejiro.

'Hello,' I said and left for the bedroom for some privacy.

'Hello, baby,' she responded.

'Hi, my love. What's going on?'

She sighed.

In that sigh, I detected tension, stronger than the other times I had felt it. I decided to probe.

'Ejiro, Nwam, what is it?'

'Nothing, Richard,' she said.

'No, Ejiro. There is something, and you need to say it. I have heard this tension in your voice since you have been unable to visit.'

'What if I just really miss you, Richard?'

'As sweet as that sounds, I know it is something else.'

'Babe, I am coming this weekend, and I promise I will tell you everything.'

'So, there is something then.'

'Yes, Richard. There is some news. I will tell you about it when I come this weekend.'

'Okay. But can't you just give me a hint now? Why keep me worried?'

'No, my love. These things are better discussed face-to-face. But rest your mind, Friday is almost here. I'll be staying for the weekend.'

'Okay. But do you promise you'll come this time? No excuses?'

'Ah, Richard! You know I would be there every day if I could. Don't be like that.'

'Do you promise?'

'Expect me.'

We ended the call, and I took stock of our discussion. I had, at least, made some progress. Now she had admitted that there was an issue. I noticed that she avoided using the word 'problem' or 'issue'. She had said it's 'news'. What news could there be? 'News' is such a naked, genderless word. It needed qualifiers to tell you its state – good or bad. What kind of news could it be that had taken away my Ejiro's smile these past weeks and replaced it with tension? Was she leaving me? Perhaps the long distance was affecting our relationship. Or, and the thought entered into my head with much force, was she pregnant? This thought was so forceful that I picked my phone and started to dial her number. But I stopped? What if she was pregnant? What would I tell her now? What if she wasn't? Perhaps the news was something about her parents. My thoughts led me to open ends, which birthed more questions. I knew then that it was of no use fretting about something I did not know and could not change. It was best that I waited until she came.

Glory had started to flirt with me in the office. Perhaps the mistake I made was that I praised the way she dressed one day. Glory was tall and she had a full-body that made anything she wore flattering. On the day I complimented her dressing, she had worn a powder pink coloured top and a brown skirt, completed with charcoal black wedge shoes. She looked quite exquisite that day and I found myself comparing her with Ejiro. It seemed to me that both of them were at par. But I knew that I should not compare. I knew that no woman should be more than Ejiro in my eyes, especially when I've known her depths and quenched the thirst of desire. That morning, I played with Glory's name, calling her Glory, Glory, Glorious, Glamorous Glittering Glory. I told her that she looked glorious. She smiled, did a twirl, and click-clacked out of my office. I've been receiving subtle advances since then.

I thought of telling Nelly about my dilemma, but I did not. I didn't want him to tell me that I brought it on myself, that I should have kept the respectful distance between Glory and me. I thought of getting a portrait of Ejiro and putting it on my desk, hoping that Glory would get it. The thought entered my mind that I needed Glory to be at her optimum. She was my secretary, and I couldn't afford a bad relationship with her. What if I addressed the matter head-on? What if I called her into the office and had a candid discussion with her? Would it make me feel weak? Would she give responses that would make me seem like a fool? Would I be pre-empting her? Maybe I should wear a ring. But wouldn't that be a lie? I mauled over these thoughts while I drove to the office. I became so distracted that I ran a red light and nearly caused an accident. I stopped to apologise, but the people concerned drove on quickly, leaving me curses as a souvenir.

Glory met me with a smile and a cup of coffee as I stepped into my office. She took my bag and adjusted a few creases on my shirt. I noticed that she looked as beautiful as ever. Her scent was familiar – the smell of roses. I walked in and muttered my thanks. Without announcement, she planted a peck on my cheeks. I stood dumbfounded, thinking of how to respond to this brazen flirting. She kissed me full on the mouth, and despite myself, my lips parted, and my tongue found hers. When the kiss ended, almost a full minute later, Glory muttered some apologies and stepped out of my office. I sat stunned for some time and wondered what I would do. About thirty minutes later, she came in again and announced that my supervisor would like to see me in his office immediately. I dismissed her with a wave of the hand and quickly went to my boss's office.

'Good morning, sir,' I greeted when I entered the office.

'Good morning, Richard.'

My boss's office was similar to mine, only larger. Also, he had two secretaries. Apart from that, his furniture was the same as mine. I also knew that his salary was significantly higher than mine. I knew too that, unlike me, my supervisor could recommend that someone be fired. I had heard that he had used this power on a few occasions.

'There has been a leak in one of our pipelines in Ogoni. I will be leading a team there for repairs and an investigation of what else might have gone amiss. This might take a week, maybe more, and I need you to take charge here. You have had a month to settle in, and I hope I can count on you with the goings-on around here.'

'Yes, you can, sir.'

'Good. I say this because you seem a little distracted. I need you to focus while I am away. Please put together your schedule for next week and bring it to me before the close of work today. Also, I'll require you to write a daily report of all activities during my absence.'

'Yes, sir.'

He rose. I did too.

'Richard,' he called as I got to the door.

'Sir,' I answered, turning.

'Be careful with that secretary of yours; she seems to have taken a shine to you. I trust you are a responsible man.'

'I am, sir. Thank you.'

As I returned to the office, I thought about what it meant to have the department for the whole week. I had to schedule maintenance and monitor it with the few men who would be on ground. However, I also knew it was time to have a candid discussion with Glory. I invited her into my office two hours after I came back from my supervisor's office. I spent the two hours drawing up the work and maintenance schedule for the coming week and drafting a memo to members of the department. Everyone had to submit a detailed daily report of their activities so that I could sign it and compile my own report. I called Glory into my office to take notes, type the memo and dispatch it.

After she left, I started to weigh my options. I did not want her. I had a woman who loved me and whom I loved. I did not even want Glory for a fling. I was not even sure of what she wanted. If I rejected her advances from now, would she try to make the office unbearable for me? But that kiss, what did it mean? What was a kiss anyway? If the story of that kiss was ever told, I would carry all the blame. I was the man; I should have controlled myself and not have given Glory the green light. I was her boss; it stood to reason that I would put her in a difficult position had she not kissed me. Perhaps, I insinuated the kiss or even initiated it. What were all those compliments for? I decided to keep quiet and let time take care of this business.

My phone rang, and it was Ejiro. A part of me wanted her to say that she had to cancel the trip, but she did not. She called to tell me that she would be travelling by road. She would get to Port Harcourt Friday night. Would I come to pick her at Waterlines Park? Of course, I would. Then I made a joke about my car being better suited for the airport than some motor park.

'Big man,' she joked. 'Well done, sir.'

When I got home that night, I informed Nelly that Ejiro was coming and would be staying the weekend. I knew Nelly would have no qualms about her coming. We both set about cleaning our flat and worked late into the night. After we were done, Nelly took a shower and went to bed, muttering that I owed him one.

Ejiro called me at every major town on her journey. Lagos – the traffic gridlock on Lagos-Ibadan Expressway. Sagamu. Benin. Asaba. Across the Niger Bridge. Onitsha. Owerri. By the time she called that she was approaching Port Harcourt, it was already past seven in the evening. By then, she sounded tired. I imagined her sitting on the bus, holding her phone and a power bank in one hand, tired and hungry. I imagined that she would not have drunk much water or eaten much because she did not want to have to beg the driver to stop so that she could relieve herself.

When Ejiro's bus arrived at Waterline, she was the first one off the bus. She stood clad in a pair of blue jeans, a tee-shirt, and a fez cap. Once she saw me, she stood arms akimbo, looking tired. I went to her and gathered her into a hug. Ejiro didn't hug me back; she just allowed me to hug her. Then she told me she needed to get her bag. She pointed at her Burberry bag, and I grabbed it and took it to the booth. I opened her door and she slid in. I ran to my own side of the door, got in and drove away.

'How was your journey?' I asked.

'I will never do this again, ever.'

I smiled. 'It was that bad?'

'Yes, it was. Imagine a maze in a bouncing castle. The roads in this country are treacherous. But I am grateful for the driver; he was very careful.'

'Thank God you're here safe.'

'Thank God. I am hungry.'

'Okay,' I said.

There was food in the house. Nelly and I had rustled something up. But I had lost my confidence. I was not sure if it would meet Ejiro's standards of good cooking, so I opted for a good restaurant. There I watched Ejiro help herself to a meal of eba and edikan-ikong.

When we got home, Nelly was there, waiting. He welcomed Ejiro warmly and helped bring her bag in. I was thankful for Nelly's civility. I knew now that he and Ejiro had gotten along. I took Ejiro to my room, where she took a bath and changed before joining Nelly and me in the sitting room. Together, we reminisced about old times. Not long after, Nelly announced that he was going to sleep.

Ejiro was tired and slept off immediately after she hit the bed. I was arranging her bag in the corner of my room when my phone rang. It was Glory. I muted the ringtone, and when the phone stopped ringing, I put it on silent mode. I lay down beside Ejiro on the bed. The weight of the whole week came crashing down on me. I was responsible for running a whole department in Supreme Oil and Gas for a whole week. I had received calls every hour from Ejiro while trying to concentrate at work. I felt guilty about that kiss with Glory. I was thankful that Ejiro had been too tired to kiss me. If she did, would she taste Glory on my breath? I was still disturbed about this when I drifted into a deep and dreamless sleep.

I woke up because something cold and moist was roaming around my body. On instinct, I glanced at the clock. I could only make out its round form against the off-white walls of my room. Then the light clicked on, and there was Ejiro beside me on the bed, naked like Eve on the day of creation. I tried to sit up, but she pushed me back to the bed and told me I had to rest. She laid close to me as we continued to discuss trivialities. When we kissed, I found sweetness in her mouth. She told me later that she had put some honey in her mouth just before she woke me. I sought the sweetness like the very air that I breathed, and we soon discovered new things about each other. That night, I explored every grove, the hills and valleys that made her femininity. Her body was a complete country in itself, and I wanted to be its president for life. When the rooster crowed that Saturday morning, we fell against each other, tired, and drifted off to sleep with our legs tangled.

The smell of fried eggs and coffee aroused me from sleep. Nelly had bought some bread and made omelettes. Ejiro was with him in the kitchen. She and Nelly were swapping stories about growing up. When I came in, Ejiro looked away, like she was ashamed to face me after our tryst in the bedroom.

'Good morning, bro,' Nelly said.

'Morning, Nelly.'

'Hi, Ejiro. Did you sleep well?' I asked.

'I did. I was so tired last night,' Ejiro answered.

'I know.'

Not long after, Nelly announced that he was going out. He needed to meet a client to get some briefs. Once he was gone, Ejiro and I took our bath together before we settled down to talk.

'So, baby, what is this news?'

She was silent.

'Ejiro, please, what is the matter? Did something happen?'

'Richard, it's my parents.'

I sat up. 'Your parents? What about them?'

'They want me to marry someone else.'

'What? I don't understand.'

Ejiro sat as still as a stone. She looked straight ahead of her, and I thought she was seeing a vision. Soon, the story poured from her lips.

'His name is Andrew. He is the only son of my father's friend. When I was much younger, my parents took me to visit his family before he left Nigeria, and they would call us husband and wife. We were kids then, so I didn't think much about it. My mind wasn't even on such things. I was surprised when I got into the university, and my parents started telling me that I should be careful not to allow any guy to deceive me as I had a husband. I didn't know what they meant until my mother told me I would marry Andrew. Richard, I don't like him. I never did. After my mother told me that I would marry him, my dislike changed to near hatred. Richard, all the marriage talks seemed so far away, and I did not see it happening. After you came to Lagos, my parents returned from their holiday in the US and told me to get ready, that Andrew and I would be getting married soon. I laughed in their faces, but I saw the seriousness there. I have begged, I have tried to reason with them, and I am tired. I just know that I won't marry him. Richard, how can I marry a man I do not know? How can I sleep with a man I am not attracted to?'

'Ejiro, you mean your parents have chosen a husband for you? Do people still do that?'

'I thought my parents had changed their minds since they never mentioned it again. And it was not until recently that they brought up the issue again.'

'Ejiro, first of all, this decision is yours. What do you want to do now?'

'Richard, I love you.' She was sobbing now. 'I ached for you and searched for you all these years. I am not losing you because of some guy I don't even know.'

'Ejiro, I love you too. But why do you think your parents are doing this?'

'I don't know. Money, perhaps. Or maybe they want to use us to seal their friendship.'

I was silent. If the problem was money, then maybe I stood a chance to compete. I had a job in an oil company with great prospects. I had a moderate house and a car. I looked at Ejiro; I could fight for her. I loved her.

'Ejiro,' I said, cradling her hand in mine. 'Do you love me?'

She nodded.

'Then, we must have faith. We must have faith that doing what is right makes things bright. Faith should lead us to undertake the reasons for our existence without any atom of fear. In doing this, we must crush any bottleneck circumstances that stand in our way. Ejiro, I have faith in you, and I want you to have faith in me too.'

She nodded again.

I remembered the first time Ejiro defied her parents' order for me. One concerned teacher had let her mother know that she followed me around. Her mother had forbidden her to talk to me again, but she had refused, saying that she would choose her own friends and speak with whoever she will. One day, after school, she had stayed behind to talk with me in an empty class. When her friend, I think her name was Chinweoke or Chinenye, came to call Ejiro that it was time to go home, Ejiro said she was busy and that her friend could either wait in the next class or go home alone. The girl had hissed, long and loud, and called Ejiro a prostitute. Now I wondered where that Ejiro was, the one who had defied parents and friends so openly, or if she was still the person talking to me right now.

'Richard, are you saying you won't leave me?'

'No, Ejiro. Let's fight for this love. I want you. You are everything I want in a woman. You are the woman of my dreams.'

'Thank you, Richard. You are my ideal man, too. I love you.'

I responded by hugging her passionately. I was grateful for such a strong love. Having exchanged affirmations with my beloved, I knew I would do anything to fight for this love. Not a thousand Andrews or a million Glorys in this life would take away my Ejiro. I would keep faith with myself and make sure to always act right towards her.

On Sunday, Ejiro and I went to church. After the service, we attended an event where Nelly had been invited to speak. In just a matter of weeks, Nelly had gotten himself known in some important circles, and he now had an invitation to speak at a Sunday luncheon. His topic was 'Youth and Peaceful Coexistence'. This topic came with the intent to state the role of youths in the peace agenda in our society. It was also an attempt to establish the reasons for violence in this Niger-Delta region and the advantages of non-violence in the quest for development and agitation for freedom.

That night, after we had eaten, Ejiro asked me about Kelvin, and I told her that he was fine. Kelvin and I had spoken on the phone about two weeks ago. He had asked about Ejiro too, and I had told him she was well.

'But who told you I was fine?' Ejiro countered.

'But you were not sick.'

'I was, and it was a chronic disease that affected my heart.'

I knew what she meant but decided to feign ignorance and play along. 'Ejiro, why didn't you tell me about this since?'

'Richard, I was sick of love, and the elixir was inside you.'

I smiled. Ejiro had a way with words.

'Richard,' she said, whispering in my ear. 'I need another dose of that elixir.'

Chapter 8

EJIRO spent a week oscillating between my house and the campus. She spent her days on the campus, pursuing her research and her supervisor, while she spent the nights at my house, committing to and being in love. I was a joyful man that week. I grew accustomed to coming home from work to a clean house filled with the aroma of spices.

The night became a friend I looked forward to. At night, Ejiro would shed all her inhibitions and step out of the shower with soap suds on her body and drag me in with her. She once made a joke, as I grabbed her enclosed to myself in the shower, that when she came back from the campus and put off all the things that people saw that made them call her hot, she became hotter and generated heat with me. The moment I stepped out for work, I became familiar with my office wall clock and my wristwatch. I stare at them every ten minutes, looking forward to when I would return home to continue those emotional plays with Ejiro.

At work, everyone applauded my sense of style and my cheerfulness, except Glory. She found reasons to pop into my office as often as she could. She found excuses to come around to my side of the table to show me something clearly. She lingered over a greeting, over a compliment, and rushed in whenever I called her. I could not avoid her because she was my secretary, but I was at a loss as to how to handle her funny and anticipated advances.

I remembered watching prepubescent children fight. It always amazed me that one child would be unhappy with another and would sulk. Unfortunately, the recipient of his angst would be oblivious and thus indifferent. I always found it amusing and felt pity for the child as I watched him wilt while his 'adversary' walked under a halo of happiness. Eventually, depending on the amount of hurt or pride, children made up and became friends again after some time. I shuddered to think of how the adult version of such a part would end. I did not think that adults would make up when they saw a friend being happy despite unrequited love. I knew that love not returned could morph into resentment, which eventually hardened and became hate. When the situation became that, each action was loaded, a time bomb at the tick of time. Nothing good – not continuity of love, not a peaceful resolution, not sweet repose, not dignified resignation – could come out of such an affair. I knew I could not afford this kind of situation with Glory at Supreme Oil. I decided to talk to her and see why I could not develop a romantic relationship with her.

Five days after Ejiro had been with me, after a round of frenzied emotional attachment, she announced she was returning to Lagos in two days. I almost fell into despair. What would I do when she wasn't around? What would I eat? How would I come back to a house without the glorious smell of food? Ejiro looked into my face, and as if she could read my thoughts, she promised me she would be back soon and that we had two days to make all kinds of memories. I smiled and said that we should start right away. That night I proposed a game. I asked that we search each other's bodies for any hidden scars. We began exploring each other's bodies in a search that deposited us at heights of pleasure and seduced us over and over again. That night, between one thrust and another, I knew that I would marry her, no matter what.

After one particularly pure and complete petit mort and sleep had started to seduce us, I asked Ejiro to marry me. She smiled and said yes.

'But you have to ask again,' she said. 'With a ring.'

I nodded with great affirmation. I would go ring shopping in the morning.

'Good morning, sir,' Glory greeted me as I walked into my office on Monday morning. I had driven Ejiro to the airport at Omagwa before I went to work.

'Good morning, Glory,' I said.

After some minutes, she came to ask me if I needed anything. I replied that I did not want anything.

'Not even a cup of coffee? You look tired, sir.'

'No, Glory,' I said. 'Thank you.'

I did feel tired. It had been a weekend of activities. After my ringless proposal, I spent a good part of the night thinking about making a surprise out of the main proposal. While Ejiro slept, I had carefully measured her finger and checked a few Instagram pages of wedding ring vendors. I eventually saw a beautiful piece made of white gold, and I instantly fell in love with it. I would be the proudest man on earth to have my woman wear that ring as a commitment to our lives together forever. I let Nelly in on the picture and begged him to help me pick up the ring from the vendor.

When Ejiro woke up, she took a very warm bath. I told her I

wanted us to spend a day out. We found our way to Port Harcourt tourist beach along Kolabi Road, where we splashed water on each other and played the whole day. At night, we returned home to the aroma of Nelly's cooking. Ejiro offered to help Nelly finish the cooking, but Nelly refused. As we ate, Ejiro noticed something shiny in her cup of water, which Nelly had poured for her. When she tried to pick it out with her spoon, Nelly turned off the lights. As soon as the lights came on, Nelly had disappeared, leaving me with Ejiro, ring in hand and a question on her face.

'Marry me?' I asked the second time.

'Yes,' she said with all sense of exhilaration.

Nelly bounced out and joined us in a group hug.

We did not go to church on Sunday but spent the day wrapped in each other's arms. We only got up to eat or to move around the apartment, holding each other's hands. Nelly had left the house in the morning to visit some friends, so we had the whole house to ourselves. Ejiro was leaving the next morning, and I wanted to make her visit one she would look forward to experiencing again.

'Thank you, Glory,' I said again. 'I just need to rest a little bit.'

'Okay,' Glory said. 'I'll leave you be. Please call me if you need anything.

I turned my attention to work and tried to sort out the department's maintenance schedule for the week. It wasn't long after that that my phone rang. It was Ejiro calling to inform me that her plane had touched down successfully in Lagos. I thanked God for the safe trip and promised to call her in the evening. I had read somewhere; I think it was on somebody's Facebook timeline that if people did not face what was facing them, what was facing them would not phase out. It was a poor attempt at rhyming, but the message was true. With Ejiro in Lagos, it was time to address Glory's misplaced affections. I called her into my office during the lunch break.

'So, sir, what do you want to talk about?'

'I thought I'd spend this lunch break with you,' I said.

She sat still. No emotion. I quickly decided that it was best to cut to the chase. I was taking her time for lunch, and I knew what I wanted to say would not be very palatable. Maybe it wasn't the best of times, but I could not ask her to go out with me, and I did not want to do it during office time. I got some cups and a bottle of fruit wine from the fridge and moved to the couch. She joined me.

'Glory,' I began. 'You are a very beautiful woman, and I cannot deny that you are attractive.'

She sat silent. I took in her plain cream coloured, slightly transparent top and her print patterned skirt. She had on a pair of black ankle-strap platform heels to go with her jet-black hair. She was beautiful. But I could not be unjust to take her emotions for granted; neither could I take her for a fling.

'I know you like me. But I am sorry, I can't offer you a relationship. If you want, I offer you my friendship.'

Finally, she spoke, 'Sir, what about that kiss?'

'Glory, it was you who kissed me,' I spoke gently. I did not want to sound defensive or insensitive. 'In fact, that was a surprise.'

'You responded. You kissed me back. You encouraged me,' she sniffed.

I did not know what to say. Neither did I know how to act around a crying woman. I moved to console her; I sat on the edge of the chair beside her, holding her hands. I asked her to stop crying. She leaned into me, her head against my chest, her halo of hair touching my bristles. She sniffed again. It was a tender moment and I felt that we both could come out of this moment stronger, being each other's strongest allies. I knew now that Glory's flirting was born out of genuine feeling and not some office excitement.

Somehow, I felt, through the fog of my thoughts, that Glory had quietened somewhat. I stood to get her some water, but I tripped and fell sprawled against her. When I tried to get up, she held on to me. I struggled to get up and then she decided to get up too, but only succeeded to press her body against mine.

'Glory, I…'

'Shhh,' she brought her finger to my lips. 'I understand. You made yourself clear when you said you could not offer me a relationship.

'I am engaged,' I said.

'I figured. Don't worry; you have nothing to fear from me. I wouldn't even have you now if you said you wanted me. I'd feel like you wanted me out of pity and attached persuasion.'

I sat quietly.

'Henceforth, everything between us will be official.' She stood. 'What happens here? I mean, that kiss stays here. No one has to know.'

'Glory,' I called as she walked to the door.

She turned.

'Thank you,' I said.

She opened the door and stepped out. I sank into my seat, my head in my hands.

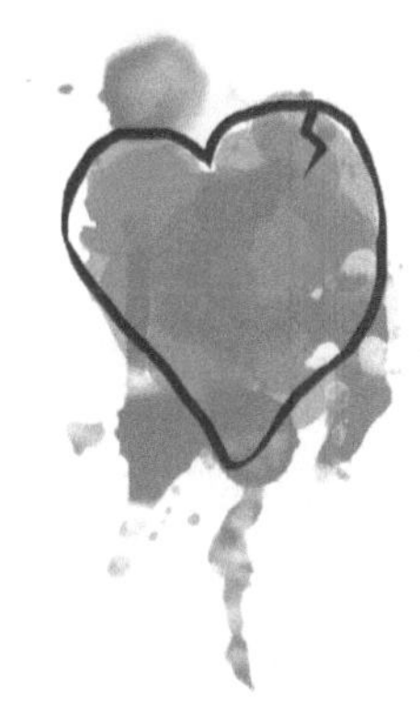

Chapter 9

DARKNESS had cast a cloak over the day. I was about to retire for the night when Ejiro called. Five weeks had passed since she came to Port Harcourt. In those five weeks, we had evolved a routine of communication. She was the first person I spoke to in the morning and the last person before I fell asleep. We tried to bridge the distance between us by stretching our love over cyberspace. I missed her; I missed the intimate moments we shared together. Now she was asking when I was going to visit her in Lagos. I knew she missed me too.

At work, I had become focused and had started to gain the trust of my superiors. I knew because more work was entrusted to my care. I knew this was a good thing because one of the signs that one's job is in danger is that the organisation would start taking off one's responsibilities bit by bit. I like to think it's a coping mechanism on both sides. While an organisation was getting used to not having a member of staff on its payroll, the said staff was also getting requisite training in having nothing to do. So, I felt safe. I would do another week at work before going to Lagos on a weekend visit.

Nelly was mired in new cases and property clients. He once told me that court cases provided the excitement in a lawyer's career. The thrill of winning and the anxiety of losing kept the lawyer busy and on his toes. But the property clients were his understanding because they provided consistent cash flow to run his affairs. But beyond courtrooms and balancing legal books, Nelly's life was turning on the dramatic. And like all things in this 21st century, it began with a phone. The first time Nelly told me he had received an anonymous text congratulating him on his new chambers, I didn't think much of it, and I told him so. When the same text message came from another number, I told him to be careful because it seemed someone was stalking him. After a few days, the text messages stopped coming, and there was peace until Lilian called.

Lilian called Nelly and asked him why he was avoiding her because of a little prank. Nelly was at a loss because Lilian had broken up with him with a wedding invitation. What was this call about? What was she doing? On my part, I asked him to forget about the call. Perhaps Lilian was trying to be friends. But things took a twist when Lilian started accusing Nelly of wanting to dump her for another girl. When she showed up at our house one day and called Nelly a coward because he chickened out easily, I knew that things had become really complicated. I was right because Nelly still loved her. But the question on my mind was *what happened*.

It took a few days of asking around before Nelly found out that the marriage plans between Lilian and her fiancé had not fallen through. They had a fight and it escalated. Accusations flew back and forth. The young man accused Lilian of betrayal and vanity, while she called him insensitive and an opportunist. Words were traded and a wound to the soul appeared that would not heal. The engagement was called off.

I thought Nelly would gloat and then become angry at this girl who wanted to play on his intelligence. But I was wrong. He pitied her and could not bring himself to spurn Lilian. I simply gave up, lest

I be accused of not wanting his happiness while I wore mine on my sleeve. Love was indeed a strange thing.

Ejiro wanted me to visit her in Lagos. It was a possibility that we talked about all the time. That I would come to Lagos and would stay in a hotel close to her parents' home. It was just an idea because we had not taken one step to bring it to fruition. Ejiro's request to visit her in Lagos was actually a summon. It came as a text message:

> *Richard. Pls come to Lagos ds wknd!*
> *Dere is smth important I hv 2 tell u.*
> *I can't tell u on d phone. U hv 2 b hre. Pls.*
> *Xoxo*

I called Ejiro when I got the text message. Try as I did, I could not coax the information out of her. Instead, she pleaded that I should do all I could to be in Lagos by the weekend. It was a Wednesday, so I had time to put things in place at work and book a Friday evening flight to Lagos. My plane touched down in Lagos at around 8 p.m. I called a taxi and asked him to take me to Lagos Travel Inn in Ikeja. I had looked up the hotel and their rates over the internet. Once I checked in, I called Ejiro and told her what hotel I was in and my room number. The hotel reception called my room at a quarter past nine to inform me that I had a visitor. I asked them to let Ejiro in. She came in a tee-shirt and three-quarter skirt, and a scarf around her neck.

'Hey, baby,' I greeted.

'Hi, Richard.'

I looked her over. I was surprised by her demeanour. What was it that made Ejiro dress like this? The clothes were good, but they were also too plain. Ejiro never dressed that way.

She burst into laughter. 'R-i-c-h-a-r-d, you don't have to look so startled. I told my parents I was going to a vigil tonight.'

'Oh, my God! You have been a very bad girl.'

'Yes, Pastor, pray for me.'

With those words, our passions reached for each other and quenched their thirst in a mutual movement of bodies. When we were done and had basked in the glow of our love, I slept off. I did not know how much time passed, but Ejiro was watching me with a smile on her face when I woke up.

'Babe, you didn't sleep?'

'No, I didn't.'

'What time is it?'

'A few minutes past midnight.'

I sat up. 'Ejiro, what is it? Your text message read like something bad happened. When you called, you sounded urgent. What is the matter?'

'It's my parents.'

'Your parents? What about them?'

'They want me to start preparations.'

'For what. Can you please just go straight to the point and stop speaking in fragments?'

'Richard, Andrew is coming back to Nigeria from the United States. My parents want us to start the wedding arrangements.'

'Wedding arrangements? You don't even know the guy. How do they want you to marry someone you don't know? This is so unfair. This is the twenty-first century, you know. Nobody does that anymore.'

'Nobody, except my parents,' Ejiro replied sadly.

Suddenly, the room was plunged into darkness. There was a power cut. It took a full two minutes before the hotel's generator kicked in and flooded the room with light. The Uninterrupted Power Supply (UPS) florescent bulb came up and covered the vacuum of the two minutes power cut before the light was restored.

'So, Ejiro, what do you want to do now? Is this goodbye?'

'God, no!' Ejiro answered with a look that said she didn't believe me. 'How can you even say that, Richard? I thought you said you wanted to marry me?'

'Yes, I want to marry you.'

'Then why are you asking if this is goodbye?'

'I am sorry, Ejiro. I was only asking what you want to do.'

'Okay. Richard. I love you. I am stuck with you. My parents will try, but I will fight for our love. It will be bad if you are scared or uncertain. If my people see one flicker of hesitation in you, they will put pressure on you, and that will not be good for us.'

'I get it,' I said.

'Good.'

She got up, plunged into her bag and brought out her nightclothes. She kissed me on the cheeks, snuggled to my chest, and we both slept off.

On Saturday morning, I woke up at sunrise. I watched Ejiro as she slept peacefully beside me and came to terms again with the reality of how beautiful she was. As I watched the daylight through the window, I thought how things must have been untainted on the morning of creation. No toxic stuff, no gases, no politics, no religion, no war, no tribe, no rich and poor folk, just people on level-playing earth. Love, then, must have been without attachments. The biblical love story of Adam and Eve was one of acceptance, love and togetherness despite their fatal mistake. I wondered why things got worse with time. I looked at Ejiro again, her face framed in a halo of hair, mouth clamped firmly shut. I tapped her. She stirred.

'Ejiro. Wake up,' I said.

She opened her eyes gently.

'Wake up, the vigil is over and the pastor is about to return to his office.'

Ejiro turned and looked at the wall clock. The sleep cleared from her eyes. She jumped up and ran into the bathroom. Before long, she was dressed and gone, promising to come and see me later and spend the whole day with me. I had the hotel room for one more day.

After she left, I received a call from Kelvin. He called to see how I was holding up and how I was finding my job. He also told me that he had received good reports from my boss. They had called me a willing worker and one that could be counted on. I asked about his wife and child and told him I was in Lagos to see Ejiro. Kelvin laughed and told me to take it easy with the girl. I laughed too.

Ejiro returned at noon, all dressed up and willing to go out. We headed to City Mall at Alausa, where we had snacks and saw a movie. After generally loafing around, we returned to my hotel room. When the subject of Andrew came up, she told me not to worry; she could handle her parents. I noticed that she was tired and so I ordered room service. I wanted to enjoy a simple, quiet meal with Ejiro before I returned to Port Harcourt. It felt to me like Ejiro had a fight ahead of her, and I wanted to give her a memory to hold on to through the period of the fight. I also wanted to make her some promises. I loved her and I was ready to fight for her. I knew that my words would bolster her in the days to come. I had the leading to give her courage in the coming days of despair. Ejiro was in the bathroom when the food came. By the time she came out, the waitress who brought the food had left. I opened the food so she could see. It was a gourmand consisting of vegetables, oily seafood, and some rice. The whole thing was set as though it was meant to be admired and not eaten. Ejiro sat, looking at the food. Suddenly, she dashed into the toilet and vomited. I went in after her.

'Are you all right?' I asked.

'Yes,' she said, straightening.

Suddenly, it felt as if a shunt of light hit me, and with it came a realisation. I looked at her. 'You are preg-nant?'

She looked away.

'Ejiro. You are pregnant? Talk to me. Are you pregnant?'

She nodded, her eyes laced with unshed tears.

'Why didn't you tell me? Why?'

'I wanted to. In fact, it's the main reason I asked you to come. But my courage failed. I did not know how you would take it, especially after you asked me if I wanted to break up with you when I told you about Andrew.'

'Hmmn, I understand. I am sorry.'

'So, I am stuck with you. This is a good thing. When my father and Andrew's people get to know that I am pregnant, they will leave me in peace, and we can get married.'

I smiled inwardly at her logic. Then the thought hit me. Had she set me up? Did she use me? I needed to know.

'Ejiro, can I ask you something?'

She nodded.

'Did you plan this?'

'No,' she responded. 'I don't want to be that girl totting around a belly outside wedlock. But it's happened and we should make the best of it. And in case you are asking why I kept it from you, I did not. I found out on Wednesday, and I sent you that text message immediately.'

'How long gone?'

'Five weeks.'

I breathed. She waited. I thought about all the directions my life had taken and how I had enjoyed goodness from all kinds of people in this world. What if one of those people had been aborted at birth? Who knew what would happen to me? Who knew what a foetus could become? I did not know the answer to these questions. I knew, however, that I was not too young to be a father and that I was no longer jobless. Perhaps the job was a catalyst, speedily bringing all the things I should have achieved into my life. I looked at Ejiro. I love her. I had loved her before I became aware that I did. I would marry her.

I did not know how Aunty Rose would regard me. I had put a girl in the family way, outside wedlock. I did not know what Kelvin would say or Juliet. I did not know what kind of example I had just set for Nelly. But then, I decided that I wasn't going to think about all those people. Sometimes, one was the only person who mattered to oneself. This time, Ejiro and I mattered most to each other and the baby growing in her stomach.

'Ejiro, nothing must happen to my baby.'

She smiled, came to me and hugged me tightly. 'We can keep the baby?'

'Yes. We will keep the baby.'

'Thank you. Thank you,' she said and began to sob on my shoulder.

'When you are ready, talk to your father, so I can come to see him.'

Ejiro looked at me. 'Somebody is getting confident.'

'I am going to be a father,' I said. 'I have to set a good example for my child.'

Ejiro smiled, 'Richard, I have something to show you before we eat.'

What is it?' I asked.

'It's in the shower.'

'Ah,' I said, catching the invitation. 'I better come and see. But I really don't want to get wet.'

By the time, Ejiro was leaving, we were both sad that she could not invent another vigil so she could stay over. But we had an agreement, we had our love, each other, and a baby on the way.

I had received an email about the cancellation of all flights to Port Harcourt in the early hours of Sunday, which I discussed with Ejiro. The airline didn't provide a reasonable explanation for the cancellation but pinned it on technicalities. Going by road became the only option I had.

'What a disappointment?' I muttered.

At 8:30 a.m. on Sunday, I was in an air-conditioned luxurious Marcopolo bus cruising at top speed and turning at the inter-change off Lagos-Ibadan expressway onto the Lagos-Benin Expressway. I knew how we would follow the road all the way to Port Harcourt. Alone now, my resolve melted like ice in a heatwave. I wondered how I would face my aunt and brother to give them the news that I would soon become a father out of wedlock.

The lady who sat beside me attempted unsuccessfully to make small talk. She tried to talk to me about a business, then about the bad state of the roads, then about me. What did I do? Did I have a family, and all such? I was almost tempted to tell her that I had one. A wife I had to wrestle from her father and an irate America been-to; and a baby cooking slowly in her womb. But I was not in the mood for chit-chat, so I tried everything to discourage her. I acted distracted, then I answered in monotones. This method worked because the lady soon brought out her phone and started fiddling with it. Before long, she slept off. I must have slept off too because when I woke up, there was pandemonium on the bus. The driver was struggling to gain control of the bus while the passengers all screamed. I looked out and saw that we were on the stretch of road that led to Asaba. Suddenly, there was a crash. Blackout.

I woke up in a hospital. The first intimation about where I was, was the shout of 'Nurse! Nurse! Doctor! Doctor!'

My vision was hazy and my eyes struggled to accommodate the light. So, when a figure appeared in my angle of vision, wearing white, followed by another figure not so severely dressed, I quickly closed my eyes. But one of the figures pried them open one after the other and beamed a small torch into each one. I heard a voice telling me to nod if I could hear. I did. The same voice tickled my underfoot and asked me to wiggle my toes if I felt it. Then the figure, whom I later got to know was the doctor, asked me to open my eyes slowly. I did. I felt very weak. I tried to sit up but the doctor's angelic companion in white pushed me back gently. Before I could understand, I felt a prick at the back of my hand. I took in my surroundings and saw Ejiro and Glory.

'Where am I?' I asked.

'Oh, thank God you can now speak,' Ejiro said. 'Thank God.'

'What happened?'

'Your bus was involved in an accident, sir,' Glory said.

'Ah,' I said weakly.

'You are lucky to be alive, sir. Some good Samaritans brought you here. The hospital searched you and found your ID card. They called us at the office. Also, when your phone would not stop ringing, they answered the call—'

'And that is how I got here,' Ejiro added.

'What day of the week is it?' I asked.

'Wednesday,' Ejiro responded calmly. 'Wed-nes-day?' I said, attempting again to get up. The doctor, who had been listening quietly to all the chit-chat, came towards me now.

'Mr Richard, please, you must rest. You have been unconscious for about four days. You need to rest to get your strength back.'

He faced Ejiro and Glory, 'Please, ladies, allow him to rest. Now that he is awake, he needs rest so that all the drugs we are giving him will work effectively.'

The doctor shepherded Ejiro and Glory out of the room. He and the nurse checked my vital signs and asked if I was feeling pains anywhere. I replied that I felt some pain in my groin. They both nodded and asked me to relax. I soon started to nod off. I glanced at the time; it was 2:30 in the afternoon. I lapsed into a dreamless sleep. By the time I woke up, Nelly had come. It did well to have a male presence in the room, apart from the doctor, who was practically a stranger. Glory had gone back to the office, leaving Ejiro to fuss over me. What would I eat? How did I feel? Did I want anything? She went on and on until Nelly asked her to stop that I would speak if I needed anything.

Presently, the doctor came in. I read his name tag: Fabian Ndubuisi, MD.

'Hello, Mr Richard. How do you feel?' he asked.

'I am fine,' I responded. 'Thank you for all your help.'

He chuckled. 'We are just doing our job.'

He smiled at Ejiro and Nelly. 'Your people here deserve more appreciation. They have stayed with you and cared for you as if they were doctors themselves.'

I nodded at Nelly and held Ejiro's hand. She smiled.

'Where is, er, the other lady?

'She has returned to the office,' Ejiro said.

'She is my colleague. My secretary, actually.'

'Ah! Wonderful. She was of great help. You should thank her when you resume.'

'I will. Thank you.'

'Well, Mr Richard, you are well now. You suffered some shock and injury, but you are fine now. We just need to observe you for a few more days. If all goes well, you will be free to go home in three to four days.'

'Thank you.'

I sat up. The news that I was well had somewhat energised me. 'Thank you, doctor.'

'Stay well, sir.' He made to leave.

'Doctor,' I called.

'Yes, please.'

'What about this pain in my groin?'

'Yes, I did say you suffered some injury. Rest. We will talk about that soon. The most important thing is that you are well and on your way to full recovery.'

The doctor smiled while fingering his stethoscope. The thing was navy blue, forming a sharp contrast around his white overall. I thought it looked like a beautiful ornament.

A day before I was discharged, Dr Fabian came into my room and requested a private meeting. Ejiro made to leave, but I called her back.

'Doctor, this is my fiancée. We are getting married soon, and she is pregnant with my child. Anything you have to say, please say in her presence.'

'Congratulations,' Dr Fabian said. 'Okay, if that is how you want it.'

I nodded, sitting up. Ejiro propped a pillow behind me.

'Mr Richard, the injury you had in your groin was severe. You were lucky that you were brought here on time. When your bus somersaulted, it seems you were thrown about a lot. There was damage to one of your testicles. The testicle was squashed and it had to be taken out. We have replaced it with a smooth pebble. This does not affect your ability to have sex; you will still have an erection and have sex normally. It just means that your chances of siring children are now 50/50. Luckily, you already have a bundle of joy on the way.'

Ejiro's mouth hung open.

I took in the news quietly. Dr Fabian stood, waiting for me to say something.

'It's my fault,' Ejiro said, sobbing.

Dr Fabian was quiet.

'This is my fault,' Ejiro said again.

'Thank you, doctor,' I said. 'Is there anything left for me to know?'

'No. You are perfectly normal; your bodily functions are at a hundred per cent. You can do everything a man can do.'

'Okay. Thank you, doctor.'

'All right. You will be discharged tomorrow.' He nodded at me, placed a hand on Ejiro's shoulder, patted her gently and left the room.

I consoled Ejiro and told her that God had been good to us. We still had a 50/50 chance of giving our baby; I pointed at her stomach, a brother or a sister. She nodded, tears still in her eyes.

I was discharged on Saturday. Nelly came in my car to take me home from the Federal Medical Centre, Asaba. It was a long way from home, but I knew Nelly would drive carefully. We arrived in Port Harcourt after five hours. Ejiro stayed the night and cared for me as much as possible. She returned to Lagos in the morning and I resumed work on Monday.

My colleagues cheered me and welcomed me back to work. For most of the first half of the day, everyone treated me like an egg. I called Glory into my office and thanked her profusely for her assistance. I dictated a letter of appreciation to the management for their help on my bills. After that, I went to see my direct boss, who was happy to see me back in one piece. When I returned to the department, I saw that my staff had dutifully done their work and filed their reports in my absence. I was grateful to everyone and let them know. When I settled down at my desk to catch up on my incoming mail, it was past the lunch break. I made a mental note to call Kelvin later in the day and Ejiro at night. I called Glory and told her I did not want to be disturbed until closing time. I put my phone on silent and placed it face down. The day must not pass without me being productive. I closed an hour late, but I was satisfied that I had gone through my work backlog. As I drove home, I listened to the evening news on Wazobia FM, 94.1. I enjoyed listening to the Igbo-accented pidgin English that the OAPs spoke. Presently, the newscaster was reading the news.

Federal Government don yarn say dem go do all the road wey dey inside South-South and South-East for we country, Obodo Nigeria. Dey talk say make people get patient as all the killi-killi and accident wey dey happen for de road because of accident go soon stop. People even talk say na because of bad road all de militant and cultist no stop to dey kpake for inside we road. D oga kpata-kpata of we country wen e be our presido don yarn say the kidnappings and killings by herdsmen and bandits especially for Abuja-Kaduna road go stop just na just na. E come talk say uniform people for up wen dem dey call Airforce don buy better fighter helicopters for air patrol and surveillance to fish out criminals from their hideouts.

I muttered in a parody as the news continued.

The ongoing suicide from young people wen dem take dey take their own lives don too much for the country. Dem come yarn say another boy don kill himself for Amasoma River for Bayelsa State because say e fail UTME/JAMB exams the third time. This one follow the girl wen she kill herself last week with Sniper poison bcos her boyfriend wen dem don date for five year dump am.

Are they for real? How could one take their own life because they did not pass an examination? Or someone else taking her life because her boyfriend dumped her? I soliloquised on these as I approached a busy junction. Deep down in my mind, I had thought that Ejiro and I could do the same, premise upon the feelings rocking us. In another vein, I had thought that such an episode should never come to pass. Suicide is evil and should neither be contemplated nor encouraged in any sane society. At this point, I could still hear the news from Wazobia FM. I turned off the radio. The news disgusted me. How many more people needed to die before the government moved from making promises to fulfilling its promises. I had survived an accident in which fourteen people lost their lives. We deserve better; our leaders had to do better. It was high time basic amenities stopped being the stuff of campaign promises. Basic amenities belong to the citizenry by right.

I drove home in relative silence, pierced only by the shrill sounds of vehicle horns. When I got home, I quickly picked up my phone to call Ejiro. She had called three times. I knew she would be anxious.

'Hello, Ejiro.'

'Ah, hello. Darling, how are you? Why haven't you been picking my calls? Are you okay?'

'Yes, Ejiro. I am okay. I needed to catch up on work at the office.'

'Richard, Andrew arrived in Nigeria today. My father says I have to see him. His family is bringing wine to my father next week.'

My heart sank into the pit of my stomach.

'Richard, are you there?'

'Yes, Ejiro. I am here.'

'What should I do?'

'What do you mean you have to see him?'

'Richard, my father says I have to go out with him and get to know him.'

'You have to be strong, Ejiro. Don't forget we have a baby on the way. Please be smart and don't complicate things.'

'I am not scared, Richard. I just wanted you to know. I'll be fine.'

'All right, then. Let me know how it goes.'

I dropped the call. The truth is, I did not know what to do, and Ejiro seemed to have let me off easily. I needed help. I realised that I had not sought any advice since my dalliance with Ejiro began. Perhaps, it was time to seek advice. I would call Kelvin and then Aunty Rose.

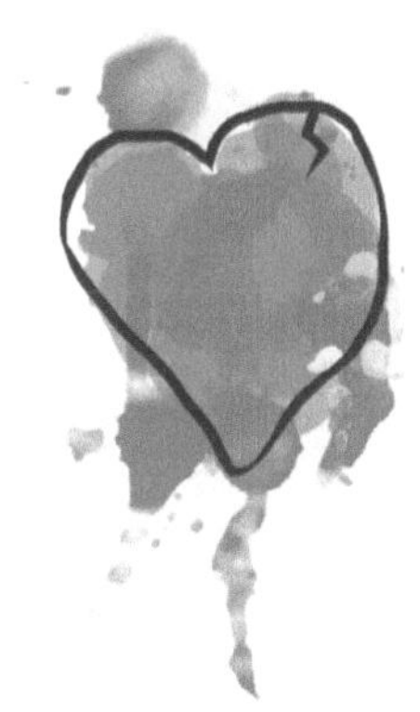

Chapter 10

I resumed work the next day, but I couldn't go out for any supervision because my thoughts were preoccupied with Ejiro's planned outing. When Ejiro is determined to do anything, it was pointless trying to stop her, especially now that she had vowed to remove anything that threatened to separate us. I had no idea what she planned, and I did not know how to ask her. What do I do to salvage this love that had been so long in coming? A lot of unanswered questions went through my mind. Why would Ejiro's parents, with all their learning and exposure, force their daughter to marry someone she did not know, not to talk of love? I bowed my head and did not know when Glory came in.

'Erm…,' she cleared her throat.

I looked up sharply.

'Is everything all right, sir?' she asked.

'Everything is fine,' I said. 'What do you need?'

'Sir, everything is not fine. I have been here for a while and you have been talking to yourself the whole time.'

'So you heard all I said?'

'All of it, sir. I think I can help you. I know Andrew.'

'You do?'

'I do, sir.'

'Glory, I am sorry for all that's happened between us…'

'Sir, you owe me nothing. And these events you refer to now, it's a chapter, long closed. I do not intend to bring it up, and I hope you won't. Nothing that happens in this office between us is tied to it.'

'Okay.'

'Sir, can you please go back to being the boss and let me be of help?'

'Yes,' I said.

'Andrew was my fiancé. He promised to marry me the moment he was through with his second degree abroad. The last time he was in the country, he introduced me to his parents. They rejected me and called me a lowlife and a gold-digger. His mother said I was running after her son because of his money and impending inheritance. I was so hurt because I had genuine feelings for him. After crying for a week, I called Andrew to ask him what he wanted to do. He told me he could not defy his parents' order; he eventually took their side. He even told me that his mother said they had found someone very special for him. I asked him what he wanted to do but he did not answer. Instead, he asked me if I wanted him to disobey his parents. I could not believe it. The coward!'

I was shocked. But I had enough presence of mind to pass Glory some tissue to clean the tears that stood in her eyes.

'So, how do you know it's the same Andrew?'

'I know Ejiro. I had seen her picture on Andrew's phone when I snooped around to find out who the special person was.'

'So, Glory, you know this guy. What do you suggest I do?'

'Sir, take your fiancée away from Lagos and bring her here to Port Harcourt, where her parents will never have to see her until after she has given birth to your baby. After that, conduct a court marriage using the child as evidence for your claims on Ejiro.'

She watched the door and continued, but this time with silent whispers as if someone was in her office listening to her conversation with me. 'Andrew respects the law so much because of his long stay abroad and he will not make any trouble. The child will then constitute a joyless complication to him and his parents' plans.'

'Thank you, Glory.'

'Yes, sir.'

Glory left my office with the file she had come to take. I wasn't sure what to make of the conversation I just had with Glory. What did Glory want? Why was she doing this? Did she want to use me to get at Andrew?' The more questions I asked, the more confused I became. I picked up my phone and dialled Ejiro's digits, but the call did not connect. After three futile efforts, I gave up and leaned back in my chair. All was totally silent. The only sound in my office, at that point, was the hum of the LG split unit air conditioner hung in the wall of my office. It signalled the cool breeze of a dark night of a harmattan season with drops of heavy dews.

Four days later, I still could not reach Ejiro. What had happened? Had Andrew's family brought wine to her father? I decided to go to Lagos by the weekend. Ejiro was mine in ways that no one could know. She was carrying my baby. I had to protect her. I told Glory I was going to Lagos.

'Sir, do you really need to go?' she asked pleadingly.

'Yes,' I said. 'I can't just hide out here and believe that my wife and baby will come back to me,' I said and stressed the words 'wife and baby'.

'Okay, sir. But can I say something before you go?'

'I'm listening.'

'Be careful, sir. Andrew is not easy.'

'I am not unaware of the risk I am about to take. But this is the right thing to do. And I will do it. I have already lost her once and that was a mistake. Now she is pregnant without us being married, and that, too, should have been prevented. Now, I can't let her go again or allow my child to be raised by another man.'

Glory opened her mouth to say something, but no words came out. I left the office and drove home. At home, I met Nelly and told him what had happened and my plan to go to Lagos.

'Ejiro called me a while ago. She said she does not want to communicate with you for now, but I should also tell you to be strong. She asked me to tell you not to worry, that she wanted to sort somethings out.'

'Did she say what it was she wanted to do?'

Nelly shook his head.

'How about my baby? Is he doing okay?'

'Richard, Ejiro is fine. She doesn't want to speak with you because she is closely chaperoned. Her family does not want her to leave Lagos until the marital rites with Andrew have been done.'

When I heard that, I wish I could fly to Lagos at the speed of light.

'As it stands, Richard, you have a right to Ejiro. But there is also a way to fight for something that belongs to you. You may be right and adopt a wrong method of fighting for your right. If that happens, the law will prove you wrong despite your good intentions.'

'Thanks, Nelly. I will go to Lagos first thing tomorrow morning. I have booked my flight already. Can you please drive me to the airport?'

'Yes,' Nelly agreed.

My plane touched down at about 8:50 in the morning, exactly fifty minutes after we lifted off in Port Harcourt. Quickly, I called a cab and gave the driver Ejiro's address. We were driving into Ejiro's estate when I saw an unusual car. It was a Porsche Panamera, and my eyes followed it. Suddenly, through the side mirror, I sighted Ejiro inside the car. I quickly asked the cab driver to turn around and follow the car. Ejiro must have seen me because as I asked the driver to follow, my phone beeped.

It was a message from Ejiro:

Are you the one behind us? If yes, just flashback, but don't attempt to call.

I beeped her number once to let her know that I was the one behind her car. After I beeped her, she sent me another text message:

Richard, tinz r a li2 complicated here. Dat's y I av not bn able 2 reach u directly. Return 2 ur hotel, & meet us at D'Ruth's Hotel, tomorrow at 10 p.m.'

Alryt, see u dere. I'm stayin @ d usual plc. Maybe we can talk on fone later 2day.

I texted back and asked the driver to drive past the Porsche and head to Lagos Travel Inn. At the hotel, I ordered some food but lost my appetite and could not eat. I recalled the last time I was in Lagos and in the same hotel. I recalled the beautiful time I spent with Ejiro. I remembered my accident and the fact that I had lost one testicle. I had not really grieved over that loss. I remembered that my hope for childbearing rested mostly on the one child nestling within Ejiro's womb. I realised that I could not let anything happen to both mother and child.

'No. It cannot be,' I muttered. The thought became really strong and I started to punch my right left palm with my right fist.

'It cannot be!' With each punch, my anger swelled and I could have hurt myself or punched a wall if my phone had not rung. It was Glory. I picked.

'Hello,' I said.

'Hello, sir,' Glory responded.

'How is everything? How is the office?'

'Everything is fine here, sir. Some documents came in for you to sign yesterday after you left. I opened them and saw that they could be done early on Monday morning. They are files for the generator plant materials. They need to be signed and sent to the admin for ratification. I hope you would have come back, sir.'

'Yes,' I responded without much conviction.

'Okay, sir.'

'Thank you.' I exhaled.

Glory was such a wonderful creature, making sure there were no slip-ups at work and that all bases were covered. I would find a way to reward her. I was sometimes dumbfounded that despite our history, no one could suspect anything happened between us.

I needed to take in some fresh air, so I headed to the hotel's restaurant and lounge. I asked for some mineral water and sat quietly, drinking. Someone touched me. I looked up. It was Olamide, an old friend from university.

'Riche, Riche!' He hailed.

'Ola-mighty!' I hailed with all the enthusiasm I could mutter.

'My man, where have you been?' He said, settling down. 'Aha, how is life with you?

'My brother, I dey o. What's up now? Have you been in Lagos all this while?'

'Yes, o. We are rocking this city.'

'Hmmn,' I chuckled. I beckoned on the barman and asked

him to bring a double scotch for my friend. Olamide was always a merrymaker. I remembered our final paper at the university and we all came in white tee-shirts. After the exam, markers suddenly appeared and the signing out started. I remembered how Olamide went boldly writing in front of girls' tee shirts, on their breasts, '4Get Me Not'. I remembered how all the girls giggled and humoured him. I remembered how he poured a whole bucket of water on my body as I ran towards Kelvin's car, and how I could not be angry with him because he was a delightful person and it was a day of joy. The drinks arrived.

'So, Richard. What are you doing in Lagos? I thought you went to Sierra Leone with your friend, Kelvin,' Olamide asked.

'Yes, I did. But it was just for a visit. I am in Nigeria. I work with Supreme Oil and Gas in Port Harcourt,' I responded.

'Great! My man is balling,' he said. He had not lost his youthful zest.

'How about you? What do you do now?'

'I work for an engineering consortium here in Lagos. Engincorp. Have you heard of it?'

'Not really,' I said.

'Yeah. It's not a loud company because they are background players, but behind every major engineering and building feat in this country, trace it, our name is there.'

'Wow,' I said. 'Great stuff!

'And things are about to get bigger. My boss's son returned from the United States after years of studying there. Things are about to get specialised. If things go well, I might even be promoted. You may be looking at the next Head of Engineering.'

'Wow! Congrats, man.'

'But wait, you said you work in Port Harcourt. What are you doing in Lagos?'

'I came to take care of some things.'

'Oh, okay. That sounds like some personal business. Anyway, I'm just rocking this Lagos. If you need anything or help to get around, just holla at your boy,' he said, giving me his card.

I took the card. 'Thanks. I will.'

'I have to get going,' he said, downing his scotch. 'I am organising a party for my boss's son at D'Ruth's in V. I. It's some kind of proposal and bachelor's eve at the same time.'

I looked up. 'Did you say D'Ruth's Hotel in Victoria Island?'

'Yes. Do you know the hotel?' Olamide asked.

'No. Sounds familiar, though. This your boss's son, what is his name?'

'Andrew. Really fine guy. He is organising this surprise pre-engagement party for his babe. He wants to give her a ring and do a bachelor's eve at the same time. He is getting married soon.'

'Wow, you seem to have your hands full.'

'Yes. But it's a good full.'

'Can I come to this party?'

'I'm not sure. It's an exclusive event. But call me. I'll see if something can be arranged. It's tomorrow.'

'Thanks, Olamide.'

'Nothing to it, my brother. We are just rocking this Lagos.'

We shook hands without Covid-19 imaginations, clicked fingers, and he left.

The next night, I arrived at the venue of the party. D'Ruth's Hotel stood regal on its corner of Victoria Island, the playground of the Lagos elite. VI was like an island on its own, different from the rest of Lagos. Connected to the mainland by the Carter Bridge, the Eko Bridge, or the Third Mainland Bridge, it has some of the finest old and new architecture in Lagos. Old and new money mingled on the island, shaking hands with international brands. Buildings bathed in neon signs hugged the skies. I heard that there were stores and shops there where things could only be paid for in dollars. D'Ruth's Hotel was built on an expansive plots of land on a quiet and well-tarred street, maintaining its pride of place on this prime piece of God's earth touching the ocean.

'Good evening,' a bouncer as wide as a wall greeted me. 'Invitation, please.'

'Er…'

'It's okay. He is with me.'

I looked up. It was Olamide. The bouncers stepped aside.

Once I stepped into the hall, it was obvious that this was no ordinary party. Everything - the lights, decoration, drinks, and even the music was custom made and paid for. It was also unlike any bachelor's eve because the to-be bride was in attendance. While other men danced with the free girls, the celebrant, Andrew, stood aloof, away from it all, like someone watching the result of his money with disinterest.

Suddenly, the mood in the hall changed. The D.J called on the celebrant and his fiancée to take the floor. The music changed to Chidinma's 'I've Fallen in Love with You.' Ejiro appeared on the floor and started moving towards Andrew, who stood watching her. She looked like an angel under the lights. As she moved, I recalled her hands around my body, her breathing as our legs tangled, and her cry of pleasure and pain when she climaxed. As she moved, she caught sight of me and stood rooted to the spot.

Andrew walked up to her, the diamond ring sparkling bright in the dimly lit room. He went down on one knee and asked Ejiro to marry him.

'I love you, Jiro baby, and I want to spend the rest of my life with you. Please marry me.'

Ejiro stood transfixed. Andrew repeated the question. And I watched in bewilderment, afraid of what Ejiro's response would be. To my joy, Ejiro shook her head and stepped back. As if a nut went loose in Andrew's head, he exploded in anger.

'What is your problem?' he shouted in an American accent. 'I say, what the hell is your problem? I am talking to you. How can you say no to my proposal? Is it because of that lowlife they call Richard?'

Ejiro looked at him sharply.

'Oh, you are surprised? I know all you have been up to, but I assure you now that I'll take care of him. I won't let his poor ass stand in my way,' Andrew threatened. Ejiro stood rooted to the spot, her features hardening. Almost everyone in the hall was as surprised as I was that Andrew had all that anger beneath his demure look. A few people were already capturing the proposal, which was quickly degenerating into an unexpected drama. Some put off their phones and others were determined to see to the end of Andrew's anger, caused by Ejiro's refusal.

'Damn it!' Andrew shouted, kicking the table. The bottles of wine and the glass cups on it went crashing to the floor. A splinter of glass flew and cut Ejiro. The hall went silent. When I saw the blood on Ejiro's leg, I went ballistic. I had a vision of my baby dying before being born because its life's blood drained out. I had to rescue my Ejiro and my baby. Two of the bouncers, who were Andrew's personal bodyguards, got to him and restrained him gently, trying to take him away from the scene.

'Leave me alone,' Andrew shouted. 'I am going to put an end to all this rubbish.' He pointed at Ejiro, 'You will marry me, I swear. You will marry me.'

He pulled out a gun. It was a small nine-millimetre semi-automatic. Once the bouncers saw the gun, they stepped back, but close enough to try to cajole Andrew into putting away the gun. Those who could run out of the hall scampered out, while some ducked under the tables. Some who are bold stood still, watching the drama that was about to unfold. Andrew advanced towards Ejiro. The hall was as silent as a graveyard at midnight. I could not watch in silence any longer. I ran to the stage towards Andrew. I had to stop him from hurting Ejiro. As I got closer, he turned around and faced me. He looked at me for a second and realisation dawned on him.

'You are Richard,' he said. He turned to Ejiro. 'This is the lowlife you want to reject me for? The reason you want to disgrace me? I'll kill him first; then I'll make your life miserable. Bitch!'

Andrew started to finger the trigger.

'On your knees, motherfucker,' he said. I stood my ground. I was silent, defiant. He couldn't possibly kill me in front of a crowd, and I would not allow myself to be humiliated.

'On your fucking knees.'

I did not respond.

'If that's how you want it, fine. I'll kill you standing.' He pulled the trigger.

In that split second, two things happened almost at the same time. Ejiro rushed forward to pick the knife on one of the cakes. Just before Andrew pulled the trigger and before the bodyguards realised what was happening, Ejiro plunged the knife into his heart.

Andrew lurched forward, pulling the trigger. He missed me by a hair's breadth. Blood gushed from Andrew's chest, and he lost his power of speech. Pandemonium erupted in the hall and everyone rushed out, except for the bodyguards. One held Andrew down and was trying to call for help. The other one held on to Ejiro and called the police. Olamide came in at this point and rushed to me, asking what had happened. I could not say a word. I only could look at Ejiro as Andrew's bodyguard held on to her. She stood there. In shock. Defiant.

The management of D'Ruth's Hotel locked down the premises and waited for the police. When the police arrived, Andrew was carried into an ambulance, while Ejiro was handcuffed and led away to the police van. However, I followed Ejiro to the police station where she was detained. She was allowed to make a call, which she did to her father, telling him that she was being held for attempted murder. I expected to be detained too as an accomplice, but no one seemed to care about me; even Andrew's friends who were at the scene of the crime seemed to have forgotten I existed. Maybe it was good as well. I could work on getting Ejiro out of detention.

I planned to stay at the police station with Ejiro until her parents come to take her bail. I could not bear to leave her there all by herself. One of the policemen on duty asked me who I was, and I said I was a family friend who was waiting for her parents to come, then I went to sit outside the gate of the police station waiting for Ejiro's parents. When they came, I remained outside, waiting for them to return with Ejiro. After a while, they walked past me again, back into their car without Ejiro. I became instantly afraid. I could not approach them to ask what happened and why Ejiro wasn't with them, so I rushed into the station.

'Oga, how far? Why dem no release that babe?' I asked the policeman behind the counter assisting the CRO

He looked at me coyly before he answered my question with another question. 'I been think say you say you dey wait for her parents. Where you go when dem come, wey you come dey ask me questions now?'

'No vex, oga. I go find somewhere go buy water and recharge card ni. The girl na my friend, you suppose understand na,' I answered, playing it cool with him to get the information I need.

'Na you sabi. DPO don go house before dem come so na tomorrow be that,' he replied.

'So you mean she is going to spend the night here?' I asked in absolute terror.

'No, na your house she go spend the night,' the policeman replied me rudely and went back to playing a game that sounded like car race on his phone.

I knew I would not get any other response from him and it would be foolish of me to sit in the station till the next morning. There had been several stories of many innocent people imprisoned just for being in the wrong place at the wrong time. I knew I needed to be free to work on how to get Ejiro out of the present predicament. So I left the police station back to my hotel, where I had the first of the many sleepless nights to come.

In the morning, I arrived at the police station at the same time as Ejiro's parents. This time, I introduced myself to them as her friend, and if they thought I was more than a friend, they didn't show it. Ejiro was brought out of the cell with her eyes tired and looking glazed. Obviously, it had been a rough night for her in the cell. Her parents tried to negotiate bail, but they could not. News had come through that Andrew had died from the knife injury. Ejiro was now an alleged murderer, and anyone charged with murder could not be bailed. It was now a murder case and would be charged to court.

Does it mean that when Ejiro said nothing could come in between us, she meant it with her life? What will the law do? What about our unborn child? All these questions went through my mind as I returned to my hotel and entered the bathroom. The hold-up in Lagos meant nothing to me as time became slow. The bathroom was a vision in sky blue and purple. The wall tiles and the bath-tub were sky blue, while the shower curtain was a deep purple. There was a horizontal silver pipe alongside a purple curtain that separated the rest of the bathroom from the bathtub. On another day, I would have appreciated the beauty of the bathroom and might even decipher some story beneath the colour mix, but I could not. Even bathing was perfunctory. I bathed only because I felt uneasy in my body.

As I bathed, I began to take a mental stock of the situation. A man had died. Before the man died, he had threatened me with a gun and was fingering the trigger. A woman, my own woman, had killed him; stabbed him just as he pulled the trigger. Were it not for her action, I would have been blasted into oblivion. The woman – my love, my saviour - was now in police custody. If she hadn't acted when she did, I would be dead or mortally wounded. Could this woman be said to be acting in self-defence or in good faith? Seeing she is the mother of my unborn child, would I be an accessory to murder? I was tired. I needed to talk to someone.

Aunty Rose.

I called Aunty Rose and she gave me her address in Ikoyi. When I arrived, I met her home alone. Uncle Scott and the kids had gone to Europe on holiday. Aunty Rose's Lagos house wasn't any less impressive than the one in Port Harcourt. It was on a plot of land acquired from one of Lagos's old and rich generation and redone to suit modern needs. The house spoke grandeur, taste, and plush. I particularly liked the mix of cream and chocolate brown.

I told Aunty Rose all that had happened with Ejiro, her pregnancy, my journey to Lagos, the accident, and the resulting broken testicle. I informed her about the forced marriage and the recent events that led to Andrew's death. Aunty Rose listened quietly. As I told the story, I watched emotions flit across her face. Anger, shame, sadness, pity, rage, surprise, bewilderment, resignation, and all the other emotions I could not immediately name.

'So, where is Ejiro, now?'

'The last time I spoke with Blessing, her sister, she told me that Ejiro will be transferred to the Maximum Prison or correctional centre in Ikoyi. I don't know. Her parents have given the warders money to make sure she is treated well.'

'Hmmn—'

'Her parents have already cut ties with Andrew's parents. The two families have locked horns. Andrew's parents have vowed to see justice served. Ejiro would appear for hearing soon.'

'Richard, you have not done well at all. You should have come to me when all these started, especially when you knew there was pregnancy involved. Now a man has died and you will be called to testify. I am sure that the prosecution will start finding ways to prove that this was premeditated murder. Anyway, because of my position, I can't touch this case, at least not openly. But get your brother; he has to come to Lagos. I will give him all the resources at my disposal. But whatever I do will have to be in the background. Also, it's time for you to be a man and go to see Ejiro's parents. It's the least you can do. After you have done that, then I will go with you. But you have to go first.'

I nodded.

'You should look at getting a long leave from your office. This thing is going to disrupt your time. But whatever you do, make sure you don't lose that job. Carry me along with your plans, please,' Aunty Rose said.

Chapter 11

THE case began several months after Ejiro was charged to court. And as usual with the bottleneck in court cases in Nigeria, the case kept getting adjourned for one reason or another. Six months after, we were yet to see the light at the end of the tunnel. Each time the judge announced that the case would have to be adjourned, maybe because of lack of one evidence or the other, or because one administrative issue was not taken care of, or because the prosecuting officer was absent, my heart broke further.

I was in Lagos every weekend since Ejiro was remanded in prison. I would leave Port Harcourt on the last flight to Lagos and for most of the times, I lodged in a hotel. Few times I had to stay over at Aunty Rose's houses, because I could not afford to pay for two nights' stay at a hotel. I could have been spending all my time in Lagos with Aunty Rose but I didn't want to draw so much attention to our relationship, in case I would need her along the way. At some point, I had to open up to about . I would be spending some time away from work and I needed her to understand and help me k

The news of Andrew's death had hit her hard. Though she had moved on, she sometimes missed him and she mourned his death. She also proved to be a friend who stuck close at my direst moments. She helped cover up for me at work so much that almost nothing was left undone. And as luck would have it, I was deployed to oversee a project the company was doing in Lagos, which meant I had to be in Lagos almost every week. It brought some relief for me in the sense that I had somewhere to tie my absences.

I needed Kelvin at that particular period of my life. I needed someone to support me mentally; someone I could express my deepest feelings to, my fears and weakness. But Kelvin could not come to Nigeria immediately. He had a tight schedule at work. However, he promised to come as soon as he was able to get some time off work. After I told him about my regular hotel stays and travels to Lagos, he sent some money to me. He also reminded me that my future in Supreme Oil and Gas really looked good, and I should do everything possible to keep my job. The relationship between Ejiro and Andrew's families deteriorated as the case progressed. It didn't matter that they had been friends for a long time. It did not count that they had wished to remain permanently friends through the marriage of their beloved children. It was not worth anything that they rolled in the same circles. Their social circle was split between the two families, not knowing who to openly support.I was able to see Ejiro during one of my visits to the prison with Blessing. The Ejiro I saw in prison was a shadow of herself. Her former plump body hung on its frame, her clothes were dishevelled, her cheeks sunken. The bulge around her tummy was becoming slightly pronounced. As we got to her, I burst into tears. Ejiro just looked at me. She had probably seen worse things than a grown man weeping. But I cried. I cried for her and the child nestling within her womb. I cried for myself and the fact that I could not help her. I cried because I could not comprehend why such a beautiful thing as love had to be this complicated. They let me cry. When I had quietened down, Blessing told Ejiro that she had delivered her message.

'What message?' I asked.

'Ejiro asked me to tell daddy and mummy that she is pregnant.'

'Ah! So, what did they say?'

'They are angry and now they think that all this is happening because of you, Richard.'

'Richard, it's time to see my parents. Please,' Ejiro said.

I nodded. 'I will see them.'

'Thank you,' Ejiro replied.

We barely had time to talk before visiting time was over and Blessing and I had to leave. I held on to Ejiro's hand, wishing she could walk away with me into her freedom. But this was not to be, at least not at that instant. My hopes were high though, I was sure we would get to the end of the case soon and our lives would return to normal.

The next Sunday afternoon, I went to see Ejiro's parents, accompanied by Aunty Rose and Nelly. I asked Nelly because I needed a man to go with me, and Aunty Rose because she was like a mother to me and the only family I had apart from Nelly. Ejiro's parents had been seeing me around, so we were received warmly when we arrived. After the greetings, Blessing explained that I was the one responsible for Ejiro's pregnancy.

Her father became enraged. 'So, young man, you are the reason my daughter is in this mess?'

I gazed at the floor. Silent.

'So, it wasn't just an act of valour. It was you who motivated her to kill my friend's son. Do you know exactly what you have done? I should have you locked up.'

Aunty Rose and Nelly tried to intervene, but Ejiro's father would not listen to them. Ejiro's mother left the sitting room, crying. I saw that the whole family was in deep pain. I was sorry. I fell on my knees to beg Ejiro's father, but his anger got the better of him. He bounded across the room and gripped me by the neck. Nelly tried to hold him while Aunty Rose begged. But the man was strong and angry.

'Daddy,' Blessing's voice pierced the mayhem. 'Please.'

The man relaxed his grip but shoved me away.

'Daddy, think about Ejiro before you do anything. This is the father of her unborn child, and she loves him. I think we should leave who is responsible for what now and just concentrate on getting Ejiro out.'

Ejiro's father looked at Blessing. He sat down heavily on a couch.

'My daughter is right.'

He then made me go over our love affair and what happened at D'Ruth's in an orderly manner. He interjected with questions here and there, the anger leaving his voice. By this time, Ejiro's mother had returned to the living room.

When I finished, Ejiro's father asked the obvious question, 'Why didn't you come to see me earlier? Why didn't you tell me since I've been seeing you around in the court and at the prison even?''Sir, Ejiro asked me to wait that she wanted to speak to you first. Unfortunately, things went bad.'

'So, what do you want to do now?'

I told him that Nelly volunteered as part of the defence counsel. Aunty Rose also revealed that she was a judge of the Appeal Court; and that, though, she could not do anything openly, she was pulling her weight privately. It was going to be a long and gruelling process, but she hoped for the best. Ejiro's father calmed down. Her mother had returned and listened to the conversation silently.

She now spoke, 'You people better do all you have to do to get my daughter out. Because if you don't, I will never forgive you, especially you,' she pointed at me.As we stepped out, I felt the weight of all my journeys and worries crashing down on me. The world around me blurred. And I felt myself fall into darkness.

I woke up four days later to see Blessing and Aunty Rose by my bed in a private ward at Western Crystal Hospital. Aunty Rose was happy to see that my eyes finally opened after days of extensive treatment by an ambidextrous doctor whom the hospital claimed was one of the best cardiologists on the island. Despite the treatment and medications I had been given, I still had some pain in my chest. I heard some voices outside the room and Nelly entered.'Good evening, Aunty Rose. Blessing, hi. How are you? Richard, how far?' Kelly greeted.I tried to respond but my voice came out inaudibly. I made to get up from the bed.

'Richard, please take it slow,' Aunty Rose said. 'Calm down. You are not strong enough yet. Lie back on the bed, please.'

Nelly cleared his voice and gave us the latest update. Andrew had been buried. Aunty Rose also informed me that her husband and children were returning from England. Also, my office had heard about my sickness, and they had agreed to give me an extended leave without pay.'What of Ejiro? What is the latest development?' I asked.

'Ejiro is still in detention,' Nelly answered. 'The prosecution counsel has some of the best lawyers I know, and Andrew's family is very influential. But we will keep working hard.'

'Thank you, Nelly. Thank you for everything you have done for Ejiro and me. I will never forget your kindness.'

Nelly nodded silently. Blessing nudged him and Nelly continued, 'Two days ago, Ejiro was sentenced to death despite all our arguments and plea for clemency.' It was an accelerated hearing.

'What?' I exclaimed and sat up quickly, not minding the pain in my chest. 'Calm down, please.' Nelly said. 'We have appealed the judgement, and we have applied for a stay of execution. This will prevent anything from happening until we are granted a hearing in the court of appeal. Please be calm. We are pulling all our resources together and using all our assets on the case. Ejiro was not happy when she didn't see you in the courtroom but I told her what happened. She sends her regards and looks forward to seeing you.'

I could not say anything. My mind went completely blank. I could not comprehend the news Nelly just broke to me.

'Our mum had a heart attack when Ejiro was sentenced. She is in the hospital too, but she is responding to treatment,' Blessing added.My heart sank further. I blamed myself for everything. Maybe I should have let Ejiro go; I should have encouraged her to abide by her parents' wish for her to marry Andrew. We all would not be in this mess if I did not allow my feelings to override my senses.'What happened to you, Richard? Why did you collapse like that?' Nelly asked.

It took me some time to find my voice and bring my thoughts together. 'I am very stressed, tired and feel like die. My waist is heavy, my eyes almost getting close, my body so stiffed and look warmed but I can't complain or explain. The way I feel is nothing compared to how Ejiro must be feeling right now. But the judges are wicked. How could they sentence a pregnant woman to death? Was there no female judge among them? They could not even consider the baby she was carrying, and they did not see that she was just fast enough to stop Andrew from carrying out his intent. And how could they pass a judgement this vicious, barbaric, and malicious way on a pregnant woman for that matter?' I asked all these questions in a flash.

Nelly replied, 'The law has no pity for gender and no place for passion. But in two months, the appeal process will begin and there we might be able to overturn over the present sentence.'

I was discharged the next day and Aunty Rose took me home. It was then I saw the papers.

'WOMAN ALLEGED TO KILL FIANCE BECAUSE OF BOYFRIEND SENTENCED TO DEATH!'

Another newspaper screamed:

'PREGNANT KILLER SENTENCED TO DEATH!'

On the cover, a silhouette of Ejiro in a Black Maria with an inset of lawyers bowing to the court appeared in full colour. I had the feeling that somebody was financing the media to sensationalise the news. It was everywhere on Facebook, Twitter, WhatsApp, and Instagram. I felt cold each time I dived into social media. I read and re-read hundreds of comments from professionals and novices on social media. I saw how a lot of people whip irrational sentiments about the issue. I had a course of verbal confrontation with some persons on social media, explaining my role and Andrew's callousness, but no one cared to listen. Rather, the news was seen from the propagandist view from the way it was leaked. I vowed not to confront anyone again on social media as long as the issue lingered, but I thought about how negative news without facts flies on social media. Some other bloggers saw the situation as an avenue to popularise themselves and their blogs, thereby padding the story to invoke public sympathy for Andrew and his family. There was also a human rights organisation that stereotyped the story from a different perspective and set the ball rolling in some other blogs to initiate a divergent view, drawing sympathy for Ejiro.

Nelly told me not to go near the prison for now because journalists were there and were waiting to take a picture of me. He also told me that Ejiro and Andrew's parents were in a war of bribing the prison officers. While Ejiro's parents were bribing the warders to ensure that Ejiro was treated well, Andrew's family paid even higher to make sure Ejiro was brutally treated. An attempt to organise a meeting between both families had ended badly. Although Ejiro's case was widely publicised, I knew that if the families could reach some compromise, the tension around the case would dissipate and perhaps, there could be some reprieve. I told Nelly and Blessing not to tell Ejiro about the circus the media was making of her case. I pleaded with them to tell her to take it easy and get what rest she could, especially because of the baby.

'This baby is a source of inspiration and motivation to me. He will be the one to finally grant me the long-desired favour out of this dark abyss of a silent dungeon.'

Ejiro wrote in a note to me two days before the appeal began.

The day came like a long-expected wedding date. Kelvin had flown in the day before from Sierra Leone to accompany me to court. Ejiro came into the courtroom in handcuffs and manacled feet. The sight of her walking into the courtroom broke my heart. She smiled when she saw me. She was accompanied by two police officers and a female warder. I noticed that her stomach bulge was more pronounced. She took her place in the dock.

'Courrrrrt!' the orderly shouted as the presiding justice came in.

I wasn't sure if I had seen correctly, but after the justice had settled down and everyone else, I confirmed it was Aunty Rose under the wig. I heaved a sigh of relief. Things were looking good. My hopes were high and I felt a certain calm settle over me.

After the case was called, a

Lawyer from the prosecution team gave his opening statement and made the allegation that we had read in the papers that Andrew's death was premeditated murder. He also attempted to pre-empt the defence by saying that he knew they would bring on a case of self-defence and perhaps temporary insanity. However, they were ready to prove beyond a reasonable doubt that the case was as simple and plain as black and white.

In its opening, the defence team maintained that it was willing to show that through the antecedents and events surrounding the case, Andrew's murder was unfortunate but not premeditated. The defence counsel agreed that Ejiro was the one who struck the deathblow, but they were willing to prove beyond a reasonable doubt that it was due to a combination of events that were not within Ejiro's powers and thus could not be blamed on her.

The judge asked the counsel to call their witnesses. The prosecution began first. Most of the witnesses called were mostly people at the bachelor's party who might have been paid to testify. The questions went the same way. The lawyers tried to establish their presence at the crime scene and attest to Ejiro's state of mind at the event. The lawyers often skipped the part that involved me and went straight to the part of the stabbing. I found the lawyer's selective questioning riling, and I almost shouted at him. But I knew I could be thrown out of the courtroom and charged for contempt of court.

Slowly, the defence began to show that Ejiro was merely a victim of circumstances, forced to marry whom she barely knew when she was in love with someone else. The defence made it clear that Ejiro took the only chance that was clear to her within a limited range of choices. The defence stressed my accident and loss of a testicle and how Ejiro had to resort to desperate measures to keep the baby and the man she loved. On the choice of Ejiro's action, the defence brought it down to the mental health of women in pregnancy, especially one as stressed as Ejiro. A medical doctor was sworn into the witness box as an expert to corroborate this fact.

After both the prosecution and defence team stated their case without providing any new evidence to add to the story or remove from the points they had earlier argued in the high court, the court was adjourned and the final hearing was set for six weeks after. Nelly told me that the case did not look good. He knew for a fact that Ejiro's death sentence would be overturned, but she could face life in jail.

Blessing and I sat in the court backroom, hoping to catch a glimpse of Ejiro as she stepped out of the courtroom. I was agitated, though Blessing was calm and optimistic. After Nelly told me Ejiro could be sentenced to life imprisonment, my heart sank to the bottom of my stomach. I knew my aunt was pulling some strings in the background, but I knew she could not pull too hard so that no one would use her to score cheap points. Blessing also told me that if the Court of Appeal upheld the death sentence, her parents would proceed to the Supreme Court. We were able to get to Ejiro just before she got to the Black Maria that would take her back to Ikoyi prison or correctional centre. I gave her some money to buy the things she needed to make her life easier in prison. As I went home that day, I cried. I was going to sleep in a comfortable room while Ejiro was going back to the confines of prison. How could life be so cruel? How could love task one so hard?

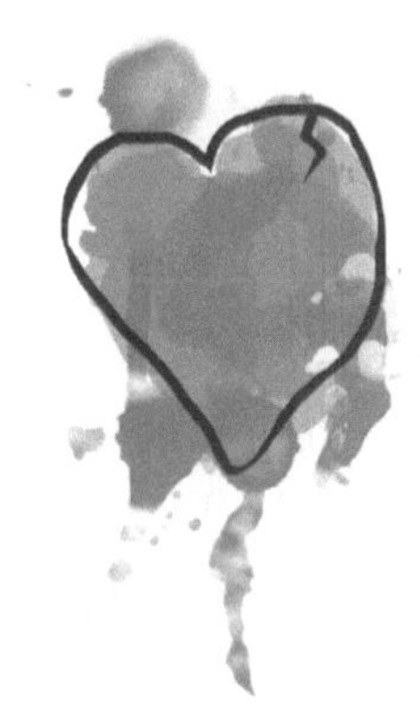

Chapter 12

THREE weeks to the final hearing at the Court of Appeal, news reached us that an attempt was made on Ejiro's life. The defence quickly sent Nelly to the court to file for a restriction order. No one was to visit Ejiro except members of her immediate family and her lawyers. The family doctor was also allowed to visit her, with the knowledge of her parents, because of her health.

Social media had a field day with the case. People got creative with their Facebook analysis, while some invented hashtags on Instagram. Bloggers raked in traffic and Twitter analysts had e-panels on the matter. Various kinds of cartoons surfaced online, and those of us who were concerned watched. It had become a national affair. The name 'Ejiro' became a metaphor for vicious girls.

The media did not make the case easy as they were heavily induced by funds from Andrew's parents to follow the case to solicit public sympathy for their deceased son. Of course, they were deliriously engaged in the negative part of the story. I knew that the bloggers did not take the time to investigate before pushing out stories that were completely different from what actually happened. None of these reporters had gone to the prison to see Ejiro. They all got their cock and bull stories from their friends and the police as well.

The press and social media made it possible for the public to become a judge over an issue they had no idea about. Ejiro's case gained international attention, and she was hailed as both victim and hero. She was a victim because she was forced to marry a man she did not know, much less love. She was hailed a hero of love because she knew what she wanted, and she did what she had to do to keep what she wanted. E-feminists took it; banners appeared online with raised fists. Twitter blew up with #End4cedMarriageNow; another hashtag read #IDeserve2choose. Soon, the online debate gained traction, and it became a matter for discussion in radio shows. Ejiro was famous, but her life hung in the balance. Good things happened to Ejiro because of her popularity. She was adequately cared for in prison. Neither her parents' money nor the wealth of Andrew's family could affect how she was treated.

However, Ejiro got tired. She started to lose faith. The only thing that kept her going was the baby she was carrying. Three days to the final judgement, Kelvin arrived. He came to give me and Ejiro moral support. He sent money to me regularly. He had done enough, but he still came to be with us at this crucial time. The day before Kelvin arrived from Sierra Leone, I wrote in my diary that I believed strongly that Andrew's parents must be responsible for the attempt on Ejiro's life. Revenge and its desire is a terrible thing. True, a life was lost. But one would have thought that a life saved would balance out the loss and keep the equation of the world at an equilibrium. But no. Revenge always tilts the world further wrong. To lose and lose and lose again.

I arrived at the airport with the Uber to welcome Kelvin. I saw a newspaper with the header 'WHAT WE MUST THINK OF, IN THE BOYFRIEND FOR FIANCEE KILLING'. I'd seen many newspapers articles about the case and how unobjective their stories were. The media had turned the story into a circus and gone to town.

So, I wasn't interested. But I needed something to pass the time, so I bought the paper while I waited for Kelvin to arrive. The columnist spoke about how the rich always took the rights of the poor, not that Ejiro was poor, but I was just coming out of the trappings of poverty to fulfil their basic and aesthetic needs. Now the rich had reached out to each other, tampering with one of humanity's basic rights, the right to association or the freedom to choose who to love. This hubris had resulted in tragedy, and more tragedy was on the way. I particularly liked a part of the story: It was an attempt by the late man to force himself on the girl, who was already pregnant for someone she loves. Luck, however, ran out on his pride as the girl was ready to fight and die for her convictions. It is modern-day slavery for a girl to be forced outside her emotional will, and I think all rich people must learn this lesson. This deed, gruesome as it is, is heroic. Ejiro, and people like her in this world, should be applauded. Also, her parents must have realised how much their overwhelming influence on their daughter had cost them.

The sight of this different version of the story got me exhilarated. I saw the zeal of this journalist to find truth in human angle stories. Had I the strength or the inclination, I would have followed the newspaper for a week or so to see what the reading public's reaction would be via letters to the editor. I knew one thing, though, this journalist would not rise. Truth tellers, like him, were not allowed to thrive.

When the news got to us that Ejiro was almost killed behind bars, I became sensitive to the news of police brutality and extrajudicial killings in our country. That was how it happened in the story of a man who had recently escaped being killed as a replacement in Warri, Delta state. A tricycle rider was on his way home to observe the 7 p.m. curfew occasioned by the #EndSARS. Unfortunately, he was caught in traffic and was still on the road at 7:10. He was arrested by the police, and amidst heavy beating, was bundled to the police station. He was not seen for two days. According to the story, he had been transferred to Abuja, where he was to be killed as a replacement for a Military General's son who had been convicted of armed robbery, kidnapping and murder and sentenced to death. The tricycle riders' family raised an alarm. It took the efforts of the public defenders and the three-wheelers association to bring the man and his story back to life. The police denied the story, then they capitulated and said it was a case of mistaken identity. They thanked God for the tricycle rider whose head was not asleep. They also thanked the Office of the Public Defender/activist, who had saved them from making a mistake.

I was appalled that our country's security apparatus could make such mistakes, that they could even think that such a thing was plausible and that Nigerians would accept such an explanation. But I was also disappointed. The few people who reacted to the story asked the tricycle rider to thank his stars. Not one person thought about the complicity of the police or the fact that the tricycle had gone missing. I was scared for Ejiro, and I told Kelvin so.

'Keep the faith, Richard. Ejiro's case is in the public eye now. No foul play can be done,' he assured me.

'Thanks, Kelvin. You have been a true friend at this crucial time.'

Kelvin smiled wanly. 'Richard, thank you for the thanks. I am glad I can help.'

We drove into Aunty Rose's residence late in the evening. Kelvin wanted to say hello before returning to his hotel. But I knew Aunty Rose would ask him to stay in her house.

'So, Richard, how does the case look?' Kelvin asked me before getting out of the car.

'There is some hope. Aunty Rose is now the one presiding over the case. Thankfully, nobody has made a connection between her and me yet. We are hoping that she will release Ejiro or give her a light sentence on compassionate grounds.'

'Hmmn,' Kelvin said.

'It's really dicey, I know, since Aunty Rose prides herself as a model of integrity. I only hope she would come up with some technicality to secure Ejiro's release.'

'Hmmn,' Kelvin said again.

'Our lawyers are doing everything to make sure that Ejiro comes out of this, soonest. Also, Aunty Rose is aware that Ejiro is pregnant.'

'Will this case not be putting Aunty Rose in danger?' Kelvin wondered.

'It will. But many people have done worse things. Plus, that girl has suffered. There have been attempts on her life. Twice. I know you heard about the strangulation. How an unknown person infiltrated a prison and got to her cell beats me. How the bastard wanted to rape a pregnant woman defies logic. But the real question is, how did he get away?'

Kelvin smiled sadly. 'This country,' he said, shaking his head.

'The attempted murder nobody heard about was the poison attempt.'

'Ah, tell me what happened.'

'According to Ejiro, a prison warder brought her some food and asked her to eat immediately. She said the food was brought by Blessing, and she could not wait. Ejiro got suspicious. There was no way Blessing would bring food for her and not see her. Ejiro refused to eat. The warder insisted that she had to eat immediately because there was no microwave in the cell if it got cold. Again, Ejiro refused to eat. The warder started to call her names and warned her not to misuse her privileges. But Ejiro sensed that something was amiss, maintained she wasn't ready to eat. The warder left without the food, telling Ejiro that she would come and get the food flask soon. Not long after, another warder came to get Ejiro to visit with her sister. Ejiro took the food along to ask her sister about it. When Blessing saw Ejiro with a food flask, she flared up. Hadn't Ejiro been warned not to accept food from strangers? Where did she get this food? Ejiro, surprised, told her what had transpired between her and the warder. Blessing made noise and attracted the chief warder. The warder who brought the food to Ejiro was summoned and asked to eat out of it. She did not; she later confessed she was paid to give her the poisoned food.'

'Oh my God! So Ejiro is not safe even in prison.'

'No, she is not.'

'How are things with her parents?' Kelvin asked.

'We are civil to each other. Perhaps, when this is over, we can see eye to eye. We are mostly collaborating on the case. Beyond that, nothing else.'

'It is understandable.'

'Kelvin, I am sure they are feeling regretful now. I am sure they wish things were different. Perhaps, they even wish they had not attempted to betroth their daughter without her consent. All these would not have happened. Now, all of us are seeing people for what they are. Surface friends like Andrew's family, traitors like Olamide, liars like the police and people who would kill for money like those warders. But I am also thankful for people like you, Kelvin. Thank you for sticking your neck out for me.'

'Anything for you, my guy. Let's go out and have some drinks. No pain or trouble lasts forever. This too will pass,' Kelvin said.

EJIRO

The platform on which I stood was becoming shaky as the money I had saved since I started working was gradually hitting the rocky mountain. It was about the eighth month of Ejiro's pregnancy, and she was feeling weak in the lonely darkroom of emotional blackmail brought upon her by Andrew and with the permission of her parents. The thick bluish wall that separated Ejiro from me was now her companion, the strong iron protector her silent restriction, and the warders had become her friends over the months she had been there.

Andrew's parents did not give up on Ejiro. They looked forward to the day she would be finally put to death. At first, they soft-pedalled for the sake of the child but stoked up the fire when they discovered that the pregnancy was not Andrew's. They didn't see it from the point we did. Ejiro's uncle, who lived in San Francisco, California, came into the country as well, trying to appeal to Andrew's parents, but they were so adamant about accepting settlement outside the court.Ejiro's uncle, with some connections, tried to see to her release through the Minister of External Affairs, who was his neighbour in the United States. As I was told by Ejiro, from what she heard from her uncle, the minister did not live in Nigeria but had a house abroad close to her uncle's. He was compensated with the position for his role during the president's electioneering bid. The minister was able to see the president about Ejiro's case, and though he could not promise to tweak the final verdict in our favour, the president promised to give Ejiro a presidential pardon should she be convicted and sentenced to jail.

The political space is filled with unqualified persons who do not have the guts to address their problems. They are at their best and have gradually gained an enviable record by stinging the state's policies like a scorpion. I see the reason for an obvious confusion that is leading to the almost breakup of the nation. He brought about forty per cent of the money the president used in his campaign. Ejiro's uncle informed the president of the predicament that had befallen his niece, but the president seemed to do nothing about it. Rather, gist filtered out that he was always drunk in the presidential villa as early as 9 a.m. because of the problems rocking the country. Maybe the president thought that all he needed to compensate him for the role he played at the campaign had already taken its place, so there was no need to help him get Ejiro released from prison.

I devised another formula to the equation by thinking through all the facts that Andrew's parents had against Ejiro and made up my mind that I would personally consolidate with them and plead on Ejiro's behalf. It was obvious that I needed Olamide's help. I had not fully recovered from the shock of the situation, particularly how things turned against Ejiro and me so fast. Her parents also did not give up in the struggle to see to her freedom. Her younger sister, Blessing, had lost so much weight juggling her job with taking care of her sister. She worked in a consulting firm in Victoria Island and she made sure to visit Ejiro at thrice once during the week after work and at every weekend. The stress was taking its toll on Blessing too, but she loved her sister and was ready to do anything for Ejiro to regain her freedom. Nelly and Aunty Rose were the only surviving hope I had to get Ejiro back to me. I thought about this as I walked down to Kelvin's room to inform him about the idea of personally meeting with Andrew's parents.

As soon as Kelvin was dressed, we were on our way to see Andrew's parents. I had gotten their address from Olamide after the last court session. He had walked up to Blessing and me as he waited to talk to Ejiro. He expressed his concern for Ejiro and said he wished there was something he could do to help us. But Andrew's parents were his employers, and he didn't want to risk his career. So, he had decided to lay low during the case, and the fact that he was not in the hall when the sad incident happened didn't qualify him to be called as a witness. He discreetly gave me Andrew's parents' home address after obtaining a promise from me not to let them know how I got the address.

'You see, Mrs Rose Scott dare not rule this case in your favour because every evidence to uphold the sentence of your so-called girlfriend to death has been tendered, and we know that justice will prevail,' Andrew's father declared after we had made our mission known to him, and after almost one hour of begging him. They

were adamant in their resolve to get their own pound of flesh. They categorically told Kelvin and me that only Ejiro's death could satisfy them.As we drove off, I started to feel some acidic encroachment in the spine of my body. The shock of what Andrew's father said threw my health into a state of flux. We got home and no matter how hard Kelvin tried to get me to sleep, I couldn't. The day set aside for the court's judgment was getting close.I returned to Port Harcourt the next day to submit my reports and sign my pending vouchers. The contract I was managing in Lagos was extended, giving me more chances to visit Ejiro as much as possible and to be present in court during hearings. I was extremely lucky with the timing of the project, and I hoped that the same luck would flow to Ejiro too and the Court of Appeal would dismiss the case against her.

Chapter 13

I returned to Lagos a week before the hearing at the Court of Appeal. Kelvin also came in from Sierra Leone and we stayed at Aunty Rose's house. Since the last time I collapsed and had to be rushed to the hospital, I had stopped lodging at hotels. Aunty Rose said she could not imagine what would have happened if I had been alone in my room at the hotel when the incident occurred. No matter how I tried to justify my preference to stay at the hotel, she would have none of it. After failing to persuade her, I gave in, hoping that staying with her would allow me to discuss the case with her and read the direction the judgement was headed. But Aunty Rose never discussed the case with me. Whenever I tried to steer our conversation in that direction, she would direct my attention to something completely different until I knew to let her be.

Kelvin and I had just finished dinner, and we returned to the sofa to catch up on the news before we retired to bed. I wasn't particularly interested in the tales of woes that was showing on the TV. All over the world, it seemed the news was about disasters and killings, particularly in Nigeria. Kelvin, who had always been interested in the country, began to analyse the situation.

"There was a little country that existed before the fracas that stole away the unity of the people who had sworn to uphold same in the times of the colonial era,' Kelvin started. I didn't know him to be a storyteller, maybe because he never told me any back then on the campus, or he was focused on making good grades and so hid his storytelling talent.

'This nation was under siege by the political class and those sick bravados who had plagued the nation oafishly. They did not consciously consider their insanity because of the mass wealth illegally looted by them. All efforts to stop their political ignorance and excesses did not come to the reality of the love they had when the colonial masters told them to sign the treaty for the two regions to come together as one nation.'

Kelvin adjusted himself on the sofa and continued. He had again taken a little sip from his glass that was placed very close to mine. He didn't bother to turn more drink into his glass but sipped everything as he placed it back. I was staring at Kelvin. He then poured a little juice from my glass into his, still determined to take me consciously out of my emotional dying state. He adjusted himself on the sofa, resting his back and throwing his right leg across his left with his left foot placed straight on the floor. He continued behaving like I was a child listening to a folktale on a summer night lit by moonlight.

'Because their personal interest was not subjected to nationalism, the leaders kept on their political excesses of personal aggrandizements. There shall soon be a demarcation brought by the revolution of the poor masses being pushed to the wall. Some bigger and better nations warned, but this country proved adamant. The political party with the largest population continued to decline for their inability to settle their differences and put national interest before personal gains,' Kelvin continued as I listened very keenly to the story.

In my mind, I wondered and tried to anticipate the reason Kelvin was telling the story of a nation and if it had anything to do with securing Ejiro's freedom. I wanted to tactically and technically cut in to stop him from continuing his sorrow tales about the country, but he seemed to want to get to the end of his story, though I was not catching up with the storyline.

'Richard, you told me about your native proverb back then in school that it is only the stubborn fly that follows the corpse into the grave. Once this nation has refused to seek perfect ways of solving the interest problems which the elites have used to rule the brains with myopic callousness even to their old age, refusing to leave political seats, the youths took their lives on their hands and expunged all those who had stained the white stone of social justice and equitable wealth distribution. The revolution started, and the two regions refused to sign the pact of coming together after two century of political marriage. The bride went her way and the groom went his way, but it was only triggered by the groom's overambitious nature to always be in control without considering the bride's children that consistently oiled the family. You see, it was a nation where education wasn't their priority, a place where gun battle is considered and granted forgiveness with compensation; it was a place where the clergies pursued their capitalist agenda and where the school curriculum was practically parochial. It will not be long before your bride's fate will be decided, but only on the historic level of moral justice devoid of infiltration.''The atrociousness and monstrousness of the first judge who tried Ejiro's case constituted a stumbling block to her freedom,' I said to Kelvin.Before he could respond, news came on about protesters agitating for the separation of the nation to allow every region right to morality and resource control. This was the aftermath of a nationwide #EndSARS protest by the youths. The protesters that were perpetuating the division due to the political crisis and economic emptiness were more of the jobless graduates on the streets of Lagos and across the country backed by bourgeoisies of different interests.

'I graduated from the university several years ago without a job,' one of the protesters said.

'I studied Sociology, but I'm still yet to get a job after all these years. Almost all of us here are graduates from different institutions, but we are unemployed because our leaders have turned their backs on the plight of the youths to concentrate on social exploits and corruption,' another said.

The news was becoming very depressing for me and Kelvin must have sensed it because he grabbed the remote and tuned to another channel where music was playing. We sat there quietly, each of us trying to process the thoughts on our heads. Aunty Rose and Nelly got home from work to inform us that the court sitting had been postponed by a week because of the ongoing protests across the country aimed at giving independence to the different regions.

The next morning, Kelvin and I visited Ejiro, and she told me that she heard about the protest for the division and sovereignty of the regions. She also told me that her parents had promised her that she would get out this time around. She was in a high spirit, great mood that morning and it made me relax a little. I kept my doubts to myself and told her that everything was going to work in our favour. I also told her that the court would not meet until the coming week, and that I needed to go to Port Harcourt and would return to Lagos a few days before the next court date.

My time with Ejiro was always emotional for me, especially when I saw the bulge in her tummy. The girl I love with my whole life was carrying my child, and I could not even hold her, take care of her, and sing to our baby. I had planned to be involved in every step of the pregnancy and in taking care of both mother and child and in building our home. I had not lost hope though.

I travelled to Port Harcourt the next day. The postponement of the court hearing was an opportunity for me to show my face in the office and to get busy for the next week and a few days before I took off again. Apart from Glory, no one else in the office knew the full details of my involvement with the court case. Anytime I thought about how my company got the contract in Lagos and I was asked to be the Team Leader, meaning I had to spend more time in Lagos, I considered it nothing short of a miracle. Even though Kelvin knew my boss and influenced my employment there in one way or another, I knew there was nothing he could do if I was asked to go by the company due to inefficiency or absenteeism.

Kelvin offered to travel with me but I discouraged him this time. I needed him to be on ground in Lagos in case anything urgent happened. He agreed to stay back and my love and respect for him increased in leaps. Kelvin was the only one who truly knew how I felt and was ready to stick with me through thick and thin. I couldn't ever quantify how much I owe him and may never be able to repay him in the manner he had stood by me in different ways and at different times.

All these were the thoughts on my head when I got to the Patani Bridge, which linked Delta and Bayelsa States. There was a hold-up and cars were moving at the speed of a snail. Suddenly, something snapped in my mind and I found myself contemplating suicide.

'Don't you think it's time to put an end to all the damages life has brought your way?' an inner voice signalled. 'Drive into the river.'

'No, don't drive into the river because they won't know your whereabouts. Just park the car, come down, climb the iron steel wedge on the pedestrian bridge and jump into the river,' another voice suggested.

'Damn it!' I shouted on the driver's seat as I suddenly noticed a commercial bus driver had double-crossed me, negotiating to enter in front of me, and there was a big truck coming from the opposite lane.

The bus driver looked at me, askance. 'If the trailer kill me, wetin you gain?'

I heard his faint voice through my rolled-up glass. I was not even aware when the car in front of mine drove off, and the bus was able to manoeuvre his way just before the oncoming trailer got close. The road became clear immediately after, and I drove on, forcing the suicidal thoughts away from my mind. My stay in Port Harcourt was so boring and disinteresting. Also, I couldn't get my mind off Andrew's father outburst and his determination to revenge his son's death. His words stung me still and the pain was like the vicious bite of a matured forest scorpion without an antidote to its callous venom. My mind kept drifting to Ejiro in handcuffs and how the police rough-handled her when she was taken away that fateful night. My heart choked, my breathing degenerated, and tremendous strain caught my spine far beyond my physical powers to rescue her from the grip of those ferocious-looking police officers. I decided I had to return to Lagos within a few days.

Glory gave me detailed updates about what I needed to take care of in the office, and with her help too, I was able to collect my allowances. She obviously had missed me and wanted to hear the full gist about Ejiro's case and how I think it would end. I told her as much as I could but I realised that the more I talked about it, the weaker and more depressed I got. Since it was officially closing time, I excused myself and left to clear my table.

EJIRO

I returned to Lagos and got to the prison the next day to find out that Ejiro had not yielded to the nurse's advice to go for check-up and treatment. According to the nurse, Ejiro had abandoned her antenatal clinics and her health deteriorated by the day. I saw her and she explained some of her untold fears about how she saw the case spinning like a volleyball against her. She told me that her strength was gradually failing her, and she had no will to carry on. I encouraged her but secretly lamented my own fears.

Blessing stood quietly at one corner of the room where we met with Ejiro. She didn't tell me the reason for her silence, but I knew something was wrong. She was dying in the muteness like the cool breeze that characterised a graveyard. Blessing had emaciated so much that there was not much difference between her and Ejiro. I asked if she was fine and she answered yes, but I didn't believe her. I felt something was wrong, and she didn't want to tell me while we were with her sister.

I called on one of the officers and asked to see the nurse taking care of Ejiro. He pointed me in the direction of the nurse's office and I went to look for her to discuss Ejiro's health issues and to know if there was something I needed to do. Maybe there were medicines I needed to buy or some particular food or fruits Ejiro should be eating regularly now. I was still in the nurse's office when one of the warders with Ejiro rushed in to say Ejiro had collapsed. We all rushed back to the waiting room where Blessing and one of the warders held Ejiro and were trying to resuscitate her. The nurse took over and asked for help to carry Ejiro to the prison clinic.

I panicked. If anything happened to Ejiro, I would never be able to forgive myself. Blessing wailed bitterly and the red gown she wore hurried towards black because of the way she fell and rolled endlessly on the prison floor. After what seemed like thirty years but which was just thirty minutes, Ejiro was resuscitated and placed on bed rest. The nurse informed me that Ejiro's blood pressure was high, which was what triggered the fainting. She needed a lot of rest and medication to bring her BP down and ensure the rest of her pregnancy was smooth and safe. I gave the nurse money for the drugs and for her kindness too. I also got her phone number to monitor Ejiro's condition the times I would be away.

As we left for home and stepped out of the prison yard, Blessing shouted at me, 'Can you see what you have done to my sister, Richard; what have you done to us?' 'We will talk about this, Blessing. Forgive me. Let your sister's health be our priority for now,' I answered softly.

'Our mum died yesterday, Richard!' Blessing exploded.

'What!' I shouted in shock as I covered my mouth with my left hand as if Ejiro would hear me from the more than twenty rooms' distance she was from me.

'I am dying gradually, Richard,' she said.

'I am very sorry, Blessing. Accept my condolence,' I said and drew her to myself, her head fixed on my chest. I patted her back gently as tears ran down my face.

'Please, Ejiro must not hear this,' I told Blessing as we walked to my car.

The only hope I had left was my aunt's verdict. I did not want to believe that she could go ahead to uphold Ejiro's sentence. The following week would determine her fate. I turned to God to commit the situation to Him, but my heart still beat faster than normal.

Ejiro's mother was buried without Ejiro's knowledge, and the news was kept away from the public and the media. It would spell doom for Ejiro and the baby if she got to know her mum passed on while she was still in prison. The funeral service was a very private affair and was attended by only a few family members who they were sure would not leak the story to the press. I didn't have the courage to attend the burial because I saw myself as one of the reasons the woman died from a heart attack.

I asked Aunty Rose if she could attend the funeral.

'No, I can't. It wouldn't turn out well if Andrew's family got to know I was at the burial. They could petition the judicial council and inform the media that I should be taken off the case because of my emotional connection with the defendant and her family.'

'That's true, aunty. Thank you for everything,' I said.

I could only imagine the pain that would strike Ejiro's heart and live as her companion forever whenever she got to know of her mother's death.'Life will never be the same again for Ejiro after this entire saga,' I said to Kelvin and Nelly, who were with me as we drove out to drop Nelly off for a business meeting.

I met Ejiro that late afternoon in a very sober appearance. She heard me faintly when I was appealing to the warder to let me see her.

'Why is your face not bright?' I asked as soon as I gained entrance into her cell room.

'I strongly feel that something is wrong, but I can't place it,' she responded as she took a deep breath.

'Nothing is wrong; everything is fine,' I assured her. I told her I was optimistic that she would regain her freedom soon. She didn't quite believe me because her face was still the way it was. The sign of her face ensconcing steadily at me alongside the vacuous nature of her cell made me feel that she must have been told of her mother's death. But if she had, her reaction would be totally different, I contemplated.

'I have not seen Blessing throughout today, and I have not seen my mum for the past three weeks, Richard. The last time I saw her was after her recovery from that sickness that turned her into a tiny broomstick. I just hope she has not had a relapse now that Blessing has also not been here since morning. Do you have any idea what is happening?' she asked, pointing at the cell gate in deep thought.

I couldn't swallow the tears as it forced my eyelids close. Ejiro, in that condition, held my head to herself, patting my back that all would be well.

'Why is life so unfair to the emotions that have proven themselves quite true?' As I asked this unanswered question, more tears ran down my cheek, dropping on Ejiro's stomach. Her protruding belly was the obstruction between her laps and my face as she sat on the cell's cemented bench, which stretched from one end of the wall to the other. The mental magnitude of resilience that engulfed Ejiro was amazing and incomprehensive because, at that point, she needed more comfort and attention than I did.

'How is my baby doing? I know he is kicking hard,' I said, totally switching from the topic of discourse to an entirely new one. 'It will be a great experience to be a mother, you know?' I teased.

I had told her personal nurse to conduct a scan for Ejiro some months ago, but she totally kicked against the idea. Ejiro told me that she wanted God to surprise her with not just only a wonderful and healthy baby but also the sex of the child. After I tried convincing her on more than two occasions, and she insisted she wanted it her way, I let the issue slide.

'Good evening, Richard,' Blessing greeted. We were so engrossed in our talks that we didn't realise she had entered until she had walked up to us. She was not looking very bright, but she had to mask it so that Ejiro would not suspect what had happened.

Good evening, Blessing. How's your dad?'

'He is very fine.'

'Won't you ask after my mum, Riche?' Ejiro asked, facing my direction as she put up some faint smile.

'You know I would always do that; you were just fast,' I responded with a wry smile.

'Where is mum?' Ejiro asked Blessing in a worrisome tone. 'I have not seen her for about three weeks now, and I am getting worried. Why hasn't she come to see me for some time? Please, Blessing, tell mum that I miss her so much and want to see her.'

As these words came out of Ejiro's mouth, tears started rolling out of Blessing's eyes like a football thrown from the mountain top. Ejiro reminded Blessing of the pains she was trying so much to conceal. I cried silently in my heart.

'Don't cry, Blessing, I will make it up to you guys,' Ejiro consoled her sister, not fully knowing the reason behind Blessing's tears.

'It is all right, Ejiro,' I said and stood up. I went to Blessing and wiped her tears with the handkerchief she had in her hands.

Ejiro also tried to hug Blessing to hold her and wipe off her tears, but it was not easy for her to stand to her feet due to the weighted pregnancy. I knew that Ejiro thought Blessing was shedding tears because of her words, but I knew that the tears were because of their mother's death.

I looked at the watch that was stuck to my left wrist and concentrated on it. It was almost 7 p.m. and time to leave. I went outside and called the health officer in charge of Ejiro. The woman promised to be there to check on her as quickly as possible, and in a twinkle of an eye, she made her way into the cell and asked us to excuse her. After the examination, we all entered the room, and by this time, Ejiro was almost done with her meal. We waited a little longer before Blessing and I left for home.

Kelvin's stay in the country was running out and he had to leave for Sierra-Leone to inspect the project he was handling before he took a break to come to support me. He had arranged with his wife to see that his manager was always on-site to supervise the project. He promised to be back in time to stand by me during the final verdict on Thursday of the following week. I was thankful to him for the concern and love he had shown me right from the university days to the level of this calamity that had befallen me. We talked about how Ejiro would regain her freedom and we would relocate to Sierra-Leone as soon as she put to bed and was able to travel with the baby. We knew the major crisis Ejiro and I may encounter would be the serious and dangerously scandalous coverage that the press had given the case so far. They had tarnished her image so much that staying in the country after her release would not be an option. Kelvin promised to assist us in getting settled in the capital city of Sierra-Leone. He said Freetown is a very nice place, and Ejiro would love it there.

Life started rejuvenating for me after the discussion between Kelvin and me.

Chapter 14

BEFORE the case was called, I went outside to see if Blessing was within the court premises, but I couldn't find her. her the didOutside me, she would have been the only one to give Ejiro the strength and courage to stand firm as the final verdict would be pronounced. At first, her cheerfulness and lack of arrogance made everyone anticipated her freedom, but as the case drew near, her fears began to interject her courage. For me, I wasn't so much afraid because I knew how much Aunty Rose loved her dad, my grandfather, and how much she wanted to keep his words after his death. The aboriginal and autochthonous oneness that engulfed the family will not be tampered with, contrary to legal laws, I hoped.

I knew Ejiro would be devastated when she eventually got to know that her mother died of hypertension caused by Ejiro's unintentional murder of Andrew. I thought about my unborn child and the only one I probably could ever have in my life. I had no more tears to shed over this thought. I was getting stronger over the case, and I decided to maintain my optimism that Ejiro would be set free and we would have our lives together.

It crossed my thoughts that maybe I should have stayed back in Sierra-Leone and accepted the job offer from Kelvin after graduation, or maybe Ejiro and I should have run away immediately her parents began to pressure her into marrying Andrew. We would have been saved this long trauma and the pending doom if the final judgement didn't go in our favour.

Unfortunately, Kelvin could not return to Nigeria to witness the final judgement. He had called me every day since he left and explained how he had run into some bottlenecks with the project he was handling and why he must stay back to resolve the issues. He promised to do all he could to be present in court with me, but obviously, he could not. I wasn't unhappy about his absence and didn't hold it against him. My prayer was that things turn out well so we could come together to celebrate the victory at the end.

I was still anxious and trying to get through to Blessing so I could go back into the court when my phone rang. It was Blessing.

'Hello, Blessing.'

'Hello, Richard,' she replied on the other side of the line.

'I have been waiting for you. Aren't you coming to court?' I asked, worried.

'I will be on my way soon. My dad had some health challenges early this morning and we had to rush him to the hospital. I just returned home to prepare some food for him.'

'What! Your dad? My gosh!' I screamed, putting my right hand on my head after transferring the phone to my left ear. What havoc have I caused this family?

'How is he now, Blessing?'

'He is better now. The doctor said he needs some rest as his blood pressure went up. How is my sister doing?' she asked with keen interest. 'Do you think the case will be decided in her favour?'

I got terrified all over. I felt some tiny round bumps all over my body as some sort of cold ran through my spine. As the cold came, my body temperature began to rise. Within a few minutes, my body became completely hot. Aunty Rose's reputation as a no-

nonsense judge, which she had built over time, made me more afraid and uncertain that Ejiro, who would put to bed in less than a month away, would be set free. Should the case be decided against Ejiro, I didn't need anybody to tell me how miserable my life would be and how much strength and zeal I would lose to carry on with life. For the first time, I allowed myself to imagine life without Ejiro. If she was found guilty, the court would have to wait until she delivered the baby before she was executed. What will happen to the baby after this? Will the court hand over the baby to us, to me? Who will take care of the innocent baby? Ejiro's mother was dead. Will Blessing continue to put her life on hold to take care of her sister's baby? Will Aunty Rose take the baby in? What if Ejiro insists on having her child with her till she is executed? Will the child become government's property? What does the law say about this? I have had these waves of thoughts since the case started, but I was always quick to put them behind me. I needed to maintain a high level of positivity to keep my strength and sanity. I should have discussed this with Nelly or Aunty Rose before the final day of judgement in court. To some extent, I trust Nelly's intelligence and the senior attorneys hired by Ejiro's dad to put forth a strong defence. One of the senior advocates, who was also on the side of the defence, as I was told by Blessing, was Ejiro's late mother's friend. They attended secondary school together and the same university.

'Her case is almost coming up,' I answered and reassured Blessing that her sister would walk out of the courtroom a free lady.

After the call, I became more confused than ever. What if Ejiro's father died too, just like her mum? The death of both parents would spell doom for Ejiro, sustain her suffering and relegate her happiness. I knew how much Ejiro would want her mum to take care of her baby, but now that her mum was dead and her dad was hospitalised, what would be happiness to her? I shook my head as I hurried into the courtyard where her trial may have begun.

'Ore mi, please take things easy, everything go be all right,' a Yoruba lady selling recharge cards said to me as I walked away.

I looked back, surprised that she followed my conversation enough to understand my situation, or maybe I had my whole shattered feeling clearly written all over my face as I spoke to Blessing. She looked at me and waved as she shook her head from one side to the other, in pity or maybe sympathy. I nodded at her, totally speechless, as I slowly walked back in the direction of the courtyard.

As I approached the court, I caught sight of Glory entering into the courtroom where the case was to be decided. Did she come out to look for me? I wondered.

Just then, one of Ejiro's father's car was driven into the yard. The car was a black Toyota Prado SUV. I was surprised because Blessing had, some few minutes ago, informed me that their father was indisposed. So how come he was in court now? I have never had any reason to think of Blessing as a liar, so what could have led her to tell me their father would not be in the court? Did her dad leave the hospital to meet up with this case? But what doctor would release a patient, who was already on bed rest due to high blood pressure, to come and witness the judgement of his daughter's murder charge? Many questions which I had no answers to flooded my mind until the door of the SUV opened and the driver stepped out.

It was Fred, Ejiro's dad Personal Assistant. He had on him a blue T-shirt tucked into a darker shade of blue jeans trousers. The darkness of his hair matched the dark shining shoes he had on, which also corresponded with the black leather belt around his waist. Dark-tinted glasses covered his eyes. As he walked towards the direction of the courtroom, he removed the glasses from his eyes and pushed them up to his forehead. He spoke impeccable English in a very nice accent, which made it very difficult to tell his tribe. I remember Ejiro telling me Fred was a graduate of Sociology and Anthropology from the University of Benin.

I quickly beckoned on him before he got to the door. I asked after his boss and he confirmed what Blessing told me earlier. He told me that Ejiro's father did not have the strength to listen to the final verdict, so he asked him to come. Fred also told me that Blessing would be in court shortly. She was waiting for her aunt, their father's only sister, to come and stay with him while she would be away at the court.

As I stood talking with Fred, I caught sight of the press seated at one corner end of the court. Fred followed my face and saw them too.

'They will all be disappointed when Ejiro walks out in a few minutes from now a free lady,' Fred said.

This statement of assurance and acknowledgement from Fred renewed my hope about the case.

Proceedings had started when Fred and I entered the courtroom, so we took a bow, facing the direction of the Chief Justice.

The prosecution counsel was determined to bring Ejiro down as they intensified the reports of a charge of murder against her. Ejiro sat looking dejected in the dock. Due to her pregnancy, she could not stand all through the trial and judgement, so she was allowed to sit. The defence put forth a strong argument to see how they could give her a safe landing, insisting that Ejiro stabbed Andrew in self-defence because he was going to shoot at her, the father of her unborn child, and that the child had a right to be nurtured by its mother. But this argument was overruled by the presiding Justice. The prosecution argued that their client's son was killed on the platform of deception and due to the promiscuity of a lady who had agreed to marry him.

'This is to draw your attention, Your lordship, to the date the deceased was brutally murdered by his fiancée. The same day was the Bachelor's Eve organised by the deceased. Your lordship, I want to put forth a question to the accused right before this honourable court,' one of the prosecutors faced Ejiro's direction.

'Mrs Ejiro--, he began.

'Objection, my lord,' Nelly interjected the lawyer putting the question to Ejiro.

'Objection sustained,' the judge said.

'Thank you, my lord," Nelly said and continued. 'The accused was not married to the deceased at the point of the Bachelor's Eve. The bride price had not even been paid. Moreover, my client was not aware it was a bachelor's eve and engagement party. My point of information and constitutional order, my lord, is that my client should forthwith not be addressed as Mrs because she was not legally or traditionally bounded by marital principles to the deceased.'

'Objection, my lord, the question has not been put forth to the accused.'

'Objection sustained,' the judge replied as Nelly took his seat.

'Thank you, my lord,' the prosecution lawyer continued. 'Miss Ejiro,' he called as he walked straight to where Ejiro sat. He had taken the correction of not addressing Ejiro as 'Mrs'.

'Are you trying to tell this honourable court that you never agreed to marry Andrew and you still went ahead to consent to the printing of the wedding card, followed him to the engagement party, and made him spend a lot of money preparing for the wedding?'

He paused but didn't allow Ejiro to answer the questions before he threw another question at her. 'Did you tell your boyfriend, whom you agreed to marry, and with whom you were making all the wedding plans, that you were pregnant for one Mr Richard?'

'No, I didn't,' Ejiro answered and was about to explain her reason when the same lawyer countered with a loud voice, facing the presiding justice and all other justices in the court.

'My lord, this is nothing but absolute deception and wickedness. This lady would have still killed Andrew if the wedding plans sailed on, maybe by a different means. My lord, would you believe this that this lady, Miss Ejiro, carried the pregnancy belonging to another man to an engagement party with the deceased, Mr Andrew? It is nefarious for a lady who was about to be engaged to be pregnant for another man. My lord, this is the highest act of betrayal, promiscuous pomposity, and arrogant harlotry.'

'Objection, my lord,' another lawyer from the defence counsel shouted but the judge overruled the objection as she allowed the other lawyer who was cross-examining Ejiro to continue with his case.

'It was gathered, My Lord, that the other eyewitness who stood before this honourable court to testify have suddenly disappeared due to the antics of the accused. But the law of this country will not accept such infiltration and blackmail to our highly esteemed profession because of the callousness of someone who frustrated and murdered her fiancé because of another boyfriend who impregnated her due to her immoral and irresponsible character.'

But the prosecuting lawyer would not relent. He called on the Justices to uphold the earlier sentence, saying it would serve as a deterrent for young ladies like Ejiro who cause harm to other people because of their promiscuity.

As these harsh words came from the prosecuting lawyer, I felt a very sharp pain pierce my heart and divide the bones in my ribs. I saw Andrew's father from where I sat, nodding his head seriously as the lawyers spoke, but with sorrow and disdain. Ejiro showed some signs of weakness and her condition drew the judge's attention, who told Nelly to speak with his client to ask if she was okay. The female medical warder who was in charge of taking care of Ejiro got to her before Nelly. After speaking with Ejiro briefly, one of the senior advocates on the side of the defence pleaded with the judge that their client was feeling fatigued because of her condition. The advocate pleaded with the judge to allow their client to drink some water before they continued the case. The judge agreed to this and called a female medical warder to get water for Ejiro.

Blessing walked into the court just as Ejiro handed the water bottle back to the medical warder. She also took a bow according to the court's protocol.

The day was getting to the thick of the afternoon and the arguments were concluded. Then the judge pronounced there would be a thirty-minute recess before reading the verdict.

'After a careful evaluation of the case and all evidences tendered before this honourable court, the court has come to the final stand and verdict. The prosecution has proved to this court beyond all reasonable doubts and established that you, Miss Ejiro, consciously and intentionally murdered your fiancé, Mr Andrew. The court has also considered the emotional and mental torture this incidence has had on the victim's family, and you are therefore guilty as charged of murder. In line with the laws of the federal republic and proposed regional autonomy, it is punishable under law. You are, therefore, sentenced to death by hanging till every breath has left your body, six months after you deliver the baby you are carrying. May the good Lord have mercy on you. This is my judgment. The court may now rise,' the presiding Justice read the verdict. (The Supreme Court has seven justices sitting as a full panel. One person reads the judgement agreed to by 6 others.)'

'Court!' the clerk shouted.

'No! No! No!' I shouted from where I was sitting. Ejiro caught my gaze and held it for a short while before she fell forward and down in the dock. As Nelly rushed down to check on Ejiro, I saw some other people carry Blessing out. She had fainted upon the death pronouncement on Ejiro. I became numb and didn't feel a thing as I walked out of the courtroom.

Andrew's father stood at one corner of the yard, looking pitiful. I had assumed he would be excited about the final judgement, but he seemed to have felt sorry for Ejiro as they carried her into the prison ambulance. A car with tinted glass, followed by a van full of mobile police officers, drove out of the courtyard. I knew it was Aunty Rose leaving the court. Nelly entered into his car and drove behind the prison ambulance that conveyed Ejiro, while Fred ran after the people trying to get Blessing to the hospital, leaving Glory and me. The noise that rocked the court drew all those around the vicinity of the courtyard into the court. I saw some of the defence and prosecution lawyers shook hands as the noble profession had taught them.

'Ore mi, take it easy, take it easy,' I heard as another hand outside that of Glory patted me on the back. It was the voice of the recharge card seller who had encouraged me before the proceedings started.

'I understand, ore mi. Just take it easy. Beeni. Yes, she is your only one, but God will stand with you,' the woman kept consoling me.

I found my voice then. 'She is my life and my hope. She is all I've got!' I screamed. 'Life has dealt me a heavy blow and made me a thorn in the flesh of this lovely family,' I continued as Glory held me. 'My heart will never be healed again. I can never survive this pain.'

I saw Andrew's father walk up to where I sat sobbing uncontrollably at a corner of the courtyard. As he drew near to me, I rushed at him and began to shout, not minding the snaps and shots coming from the media outlets.

'You are a wicked man, and wickedness dwells all around you. Osanobua di gbé éh,' I said in my Esan dialect and rushed at him.

The last thing I felt before I hit the ground was my leg hit a stone.

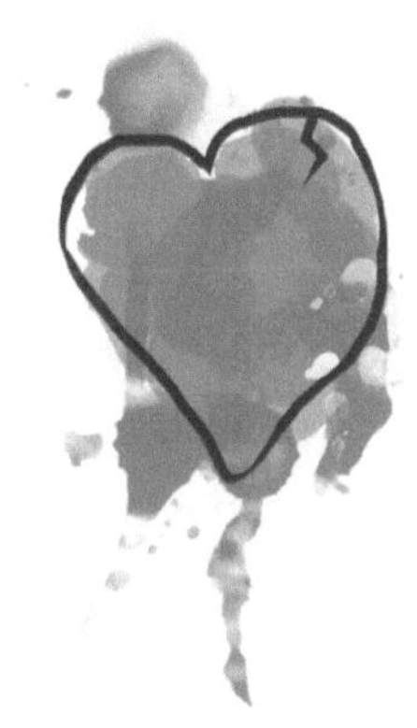

Chapter 15

I woke up the following day to discover that I was in the same hospital with Blessing. At first, I was not conscious of the people who were with me because the strength to carry on had left me, and I was dizzy. After a few moments, I was able to see Kelvin and Glory.

Kelvin had called me after I fainted, and Glory answered the call and gave him the download of all that happened in court. He got on the last flight out of his country. He had to pause the project he was working on to be with me and help me get through the difficult and miserable period.

'Life is not fair and I have taken my portion of the unfairness of life—,' I started to talk, but Glory would not allow me to finish my statement.

'You need some rest, sir. There is no need to keep thinking about what has happened. It is a situation that you cannot change, so you have to think above it and live on,' Glory appealed to me.

'You have to be strong, guy. I understand how terrible the situation is, but you have to look beyond now. Don't allow this permanently to destroy the bright and beautiful future ahead of you,' Kelvin admonished.

'I cannot live with it. You've got no idea what Ejiro means to me,' I responded and turned to face the other side of the bed where the wall constituted a barrier between the outer world and me.

At this point, a nurse came into my room to administer some injections and drugs. I told the nurse that I would like to be discharged from the hospital that same day, but they told me I could not leave as they needed to monitor me. I needed to see Ejiro. I thought about the wonderful moments I had shared with her. I recalled how we went home together during a heavy downpour one afternoon while we were in secondary school. I recalled the day I met her again, years after her parents took her away from me. I remembered the day she prepared the most sumptuous meal I had ever eaten during one of those visits to her in Lagos. I recalled the day Ejiro stabbed Andrew; and how she was publicly messed up and molested helplessly before my very eyes. I remembered the verdict of the court and how Ejiro fell in the dock and fainted.

'Oh my God!' I exclaimed in a loud voice.

Very early the next morning, I woke Kelvin up and told him I had to see Ejiro before she would be finally gone. Before we could manoeuvre from the hospital to the prison, it was almost 8 am. I had not seen Aunty Rose since she passed the death sentence on Ejiro, and I had refused to answer her calls or go back to her house. Kelvin and Nelly tried to talk to me about it, trying to make me understand why Aunty Rose could not tweak the judgement to favour Ejiro. But all their efforts to appease me were futile, and I warned Nelly never to relate anything about Aunty Rose and her family to me. I still could not get over the fact that she could not do anything to save my woman.

I was alerted by the beeps on my phone. When I took a swipe to check who was calling that early, it was Phil, Aunty Rose's son. I loved Phil so much that I still wanted to talk to him despite my anger at his mother. I quickly answered the call, only to hear Aunty Rose on the phone. In a desperate quest to reach out to me since I wasn't answering her calls, she had called me with Phil's phone.

We got to the prison, but they didn't allow us to see Ejiro. We went outside and came back about thirty minutes later, but still, we couldn't see her. Kelvin and I sat in the front of the yard, waiting to see if we could find a warder who would be kind enough to allow us access to her. Then one hour later, we saw Ejiro being taken away by three warders. She had complained of stomach pain and was being taken to a hospital outside of the prison as her current situation could not be handled by her health officer and the nurses in the prison clinic, one of the warders with her explained to Kelvin and me. She was in obvious pain and discomfort. I ran towards her and held her despite the security agents. The warders looked on as Ejiro held me tightly to herself, raising her two handcuffed hands over my head to my neck.

'I love you so much, Richard. Tell my mum that I love her so much; tell my dad that he is one in a million, and I am sorry I could not make him proud. Also, tell Blessing that I am very sorry for disappointing her—,' Ejiro said as uncontrollable tears ran down her eyes and drowned the rest of her words.

Her prison uniform had been changed to a dark blue one, signifying her death sentence, and her body was cold. As I held her, I felt the kick of my unborn child in her womb. The baby was protesting, rejecting the fate of the mother he would never grow up to know.

Kelvin stood at a distance, looking at how Ejiro sobbed and refused to let me go. The putrescent and salacious nature of a dying person was obvious all over Ejiro's body. As the warders stood looking at us, Nelly and Blessing entered the prison yard.

'Oh my God! My sister o! The only person I have left in this world is going to be killed too! My God! My God! How will I survive alone in this cruel world?' Blessing screamed.

Ejiro expressed shock at what Blessing said. 'How do you mean? Where is mum? Where is dad?'

'Mum died after the second judgment that convicted you, and dad died yesterday,' Blessing announced.

The shock of the news sent Ejiro into a sudden world of silence. She stood on, looking like a statue and didn't even respond to my tears or Blessing's wailing. There was no more agony left for Ejiro to share; no more tears left for her to shed. It was as if her well of emotions instantaneously dried up.

The warders signalled to us that it was time for Ejiro to be taken away. Blessing and I held on to her and cried, hot and thick tears flowing down our cheeks to our necks. It began to rain softly, yet none of us left the rain. Ejiro sheepishly followed the warders, not even casting a glance back towards where Blessing and I still held each other and cried. Water ran down my nose as I greatly perspired, feeling some internal heat. My breath gravitated so fast with speed and acute muteness when I saw the tears in Ejiro's eyes as they led her away to the hospital, where she would probably spend a few days in misery, then return to the prison to wait for the hangman's noose.

My heart raced fast like it was going to tear out of my body. Life became meaningless to me. How could life be this cruel! How could life flaunt its beauty and splendour before me, only to have them cut short before I even started to enjoy them? I had plans. We had plans. Ejiro and I had plans. We were going to give our child the best of the best in life. We were going to dote on her. I was sure we were going to have a pretty baby girl, as cute as her mother. Ejiro wanted a son. She said she wanted my handsomeness in double. She said she had too much love for just me; she wanted to love 'two men' in her life. Where did we go wrong? Can this sentence be appealed again? I didn't think so. Can a miracle happen that would keep her alive even after the baby was born? Maybe a presidential pardon? I tried to keep hope and faith alive, but it was hard.

Suddenly, a loud shriek brought me out of my silent grief. It was Ejiro.

'Her water has broken!' one of the warders shouted, and the others rushed at Ejiro, making attempts to get her to the waiting van as fast as they could. At this point, I began to feel some miscalculations in my brain as though I had lost my memory. I started walking to an unknown location.

'We got to the hospital where Ejiro was taken. The warders were in tears. I knew what had happened. I didn't need to be told. Kelvin understood this too and held Blessing and me. I only had a question.

'Is the baby alive?'

'No. Your baby was a stillbirth. Ejiro developed eclampsia during labour and all the doctor's efforts to stabilise her failed.'

'Why did this happen?' I heard Kelvin ask.

'Oh, Father!' Blessing shouted.

'Her blood pressure was very high when she was brought in. We tried to administer—' the doctor explained to Kelvin, who had been introduced as my brother.

I didn't wait to hear anything more. I couldn't even have heard if I had waited. I developed sudden deafness. A week later, I was diagnosed with Post-Traumatic Stress Disorder.

Kelvin and Nelly claimed Ejiro and the baby's bodies to give them a befitting burial. Aunty Rose also asked Blessing to move in with her to help her get through the pain of losing her parents and her only sister.

For me, I am here now because Kelvin and Nelly didn't give up on me.

'In the quest for self-determination, the supreme price is reasonable.'

This became my line of thoughts not blaming Ejiro for the step she took. She was bold and full of courage. She would forever be the woman of my dreams. Our hero of love, equality, power and symbol of courage. I was taken to see a specialists about my case, and gradually, I began to crawl out of my shell. It was a slow and agonising process, but I had Kelvin and Nelly and Aunty Rose's family. They all stood by me and helped me heal. I can talk about my experience now without falling back into depression, though I am not even aware if I have forgiven Aunty Rose.

'Would I ever be in love again?' This I thought not possible as revenge and justice hold brief for callous men waiting to spite the venom of unreasonable anger.It's been three years since I suffered the tragic loss that shattered my life, but I am here, holding on because they say time heals all wounds. I am here, waiting for time.

THE END

www.ingramcontent.com/pod-product-compliance
Ingram Content Group UK Ltd.
Pitfield, Milton Keynes, MK11 3LW, UK
UKHW041638190726
13854UKWH00006B/2575

9 789785 342574